DEEP OVERSTOCK

#6: Westerns
October 2019

WEST - WESTERNS

EDITORIAL

EDITOR-IN-CHIEF: Bobby Eversmann

MANAGING EDITORS: Mickey Collins & Ariel Kusby

PROSE: Mickey Collins & Bobby Eversmann & Z.B. Wagman

POETRY: Ariel Kusby

SOCIAL MEDIA: Ariel Kusby & Caroline McCulloch

WEB DESIGN: Mickey Collins

INTERIOR DESIGN: Mickey Collins

COVER DESIGN: Emily Lakehomer

CONTACT: editors@deepoverstock.com
deepoverstock.com

On the Shelves

Letter from the Editors

Hello there pardners,

Ah, the old West: a time of cowboys, cowgirls, and other cow-people. Our contributors weren't horsing around this time. We lassooed up the best of the West from east to west, but especially the west. Saddle up for a few stories, poems, and art that will keep you entertained on the range. But we won't buffalo you into enjoying them.

A special thanks to Emily Lakehomer for the cover cowgirl in blue, everyone who submitted a piece or two, and to readers like you.

As the sun sets on summer, we're looking forward to fall. The leaves are dying, the rain is here, and it's getting darker. But don't shy away from the shadows, be inspired by them! Our next issue will be Horror! What makes you want to lock your doors at night but also during the day, other than the falling temperatures? Put a new fear into us. Make us faint. Keep us up at night.

Send your horrific tales of gruesomeness to submissions@deepoverstock.com by November 20th.

Deep Overstock Editors

Rock Candy

by Michael Calkins

William Bates had a hold of the tail of his daddy's coat. They were moving slowly down the street and Willy could only see trouser legs and skirts. It seemed the whole town was heading to the same place at the same time and nobody was paying attention to anyone as small as Willy. He dodged knees and parasols and picnic baskets, all swung as if no one could be hit. Once, a panting, fuzzy hound brushed by him and Willy reached out for the dog's tail, but he remembered that he needed to stay with his daddy or he wouldn't get the treat he had been promised if he was a good boy. So he held tight to his daddy's coat and let the dog disappear among the petticoats and dusty shoes.

Willy was panting a little himself when his daddy came to a sudden stop. He reached down and took hold of his son. He tried to lift Willy onto his shoulder but the boy still had the coat tail in his hand. "Let go now, Willy. I'm gonna put you on my shoulder so you can see." Willy let go and soon enough he was on his daddy's left shoulder, above the pants and skirts to a world of hats and heads. Willy's father was not especially tall, but the boy could see over the crowd, mostly, and now could see what they had come for.

His daddy had explained that there would be something called a scaffold and he had described what it would look like. Willy's mama had objected to telling the boy anything about such terrible business. She had then repeated her objection to her son being taken to see it. But Willy's daddy had told her that life was full of unpleasantness and this particular unpleasantness was a chance for their son to learn something about the law and its consequences. He was a citizen, after all, even young as he was. Her answer had been only to repeat that there was no way on God's good earth that she would be going with them to watch such barbarity.

Willy wasn't sure what his mama was on about. The scaffold looked just like his daddy had described it. It looked to him like you could fit most all the dogs he'd ever seen on there at once and it wouldn't fall down or anything. So far in his life, Willy was pretty sure that his daddy was always right, so he didn't know what the fuss was about. But, of course, his mama was right a good deal of the time, too, so Willy just kept his head down and tried to be a good boy.

Someone jostled them and Willy's daddy had to lean over a little to keep his balance. Willy reached around his daddy's head with his right arm and held on. His hand grabbed his daddy's ear, but not too tight, because he remembered what had happened last time. When they were balanced again, Willy looked around at the people. He recognized just about everyone he could see. A couple other children he knew were also up on grown-ups' shoulders. One was sucking on a piece of candy.

Willy knew his daddy had some rock candy in the pocket of his coat. He knew it because he had been in the store when his daddy had bought it. When his daddy had put it in his pocket, he had told Willy that he could have some after, if he was a good boy. Willy knew he was a good boy, but because his parents didn't always know it, he had been extra good so far. He sat as still as he could and kept his balance so he wouldn't have to squeeze his daddy's ear too hard.

All the people were talking, it seemed. Even Willy's daddy had struck up a conversation with another man standing just in front of them. There was so much talking he could hardly make out what was being said. Mostly it was just noise like frogs croaking around the pond in the evening. Willy smiled thinking about the people like they were frogs. He liked frogs. If everything went as he imagined it should, he was going to take the rock candy his daddy would give him for being a good boy and go out to the pond, where he would suck on rock candy while he caught frogs. Like his daddy would say sometimes, "There's nothing in the world better than that."

Willy was good at catching frogs and he was good at sucking on hard candy, but he had never done both at the same time. The way he figured it, if a person was good at two things and liked both those things, then doing them at the same time had to be a lot better than either one alone. His mama might fuss at him for putting rock candy in his mouth with hands that were holding frogs, but he'd just do his best to keep his back to the house. Mama was good and decent and she knew a lot, but what she didn't know about frogs could fill that scaffold and have a mess left over besides.

From behind them, Willy could hear the voice of Widow Stanley. He turned his head to be sure, and there she was, talking to her daughter Widow Harper and another woman Willy wasn't sure he knew. His daddy had a name for the widows, but his mama had forbidden Willy to ever use it or even think it, though she had smiled a little while she told him. "It's true," the Widow Stanley said, mostly seeming to talk to the unknown woman. "If he doesn't die the first time they hang him then they have to haul him up and hang him again. And if that doesn't kill him they've got to do it a third time. And if that doesn't do for him then they have to let him go."

"Let him go?" said the woman.

""Of course. If he isn't done in three tries then that's proof that the Good Lord doesn't want him yet. And no judge or jury can argue with the Good Lord about that, though the legislature might try." The women nodded, their heads going up and down together. This was news to Willy. His daddy hadn't told him much about the hanging except what the scaffold looked like and that a bad man who had done a bad thing was going to be punished on it, which seemed to Willy like a reasonable thing. After all, if he could be punished even though he was a good boy then why shouldn't a bad man be punished?

The croaking of the crowd changed to a hum. People were pointing toward the jailhouse. Willy looked over to see a group of men coming out of the building. He recognized the sheriff and the young minister, but he didn't know the man in shackles. The man looked very sad, but he kept his head up. Willy figured that that was just about the right expression for someone who was going to be punished in front of so many people. Willy didn't think he had ever been punished in front of more than three or four people and that was bad enough.

His daddy patted Willy's knee and pointed at the group of men. He didn't say anything, though, which surprised Willy a little. When his daddy had told him about the scaffold and the bad man, he had told Willy he would let him know what was happening. But he was quiet now like most of the crowd. As the men approached the scaffold, though, the fuzzy hound ran out in front of them and up onto the platform. He bowed and bounded and looked like he wanted to play, which caused the crowd to laugh until some of the men had chased him off. And then the group was on the scaffold and they put the bad man under the knotted rope.

The sheriff took a piece of paper from his pocket and unfolded it. He cleared his throat and then he called the bad man by his name, "Matthew Swanson", and told him and the crowd how he had been found guilty and what he was guilty of, which sounded very bad, indeed, to Willy. Then he told them all that the punishment was, "To be hanged by the neck until dead." Some in the crowd shouted at Matthew Swanson then, saying all sorts of nasty things that Willy's mama would never approve.

Then the sheriff asked if Matthew Swanson had any last words. He did. Willy didn't really listen to him, because he was a bad man who had been found guilty and there wasn't anything that a man like that could say that a good boy like Willy needed to hear. So Willy looked around hoping to spot the fuzzy hound and trying to be undeniably good so his daddy would give him that rock candy. He knew he was supposed to be learning about being a citizen, but he had plenty of time for that later. There were too many frogs to catch and too much candy to eat before then.

There was a loud noise from the scaffold and some in the crowd gasped. Willy turned back to look. His daddy was patting Willy's knee and pointing. Part of Matthew Swanson had fallen through the floor of the scaffold. Willy could see his legs down there. The rest of him was struggling above. "His neck ain't broke," said someone.

"They done it wrong," said someone else. Willy stared at Matthew Swanson hanging from the knotted rope. The bad man's eyes were bulging and his face was red. The rope twisted and Willy could see the man's hands manacled behind him. His legs kicked hard. They banged against the side of the hole in the scaffold. They kicked like frog's legs did sometimes when Willy was holding one. They'd kick hard like they were trying to swim away from Willy's hands. And sometimes they kicked so much that Willy would let them go because he just wanted to hold them, not fight them.

Matthew Swanson kicked all he could, which seemed like a

lot to Willy. But then he gave up kicking and he wasn't so much like a frog anymore. Or, anyway, not so much like any frog Willy wanted anything to do with. His mama had told Willy once how there were people who killed frogs so they could cook and eat their legs. Thinking about that now, looking at the hanged man, put a picture in Willy's head and he didn't want to think about frogs any more.

Willy watched as the bad man stopped moving except for the rope swaying him back and forth and twisting him around. "I thought for sure they'd have to haul him up and try again," said the Widow Stanley. "But it looks like the Good Lord didn't object." Maybe the other ladies nodded, but Willy didn't look around to see. He kept his eyes on Matthew Swanson. And when his daddy pressed something against Willy's right hand, he let go of the ear and took the rock candy, proof that he had been a good boy.

Willy put the candy in his mouth and sucked on it absently while his daddy lifted him off his shoulder and back to the ground. Willy grabbed the tail of his daddy's coat and they started off toward home. While he was walking past parasols and picnic baskets, Willy thought about his plans. He had been a good boy and maybe now he was a good citizen, too. But the candy didn't taste like much of anything and it was hard to be good at sucking on it when it didn't taste so good. And that was a shame, because now he wouldn't have anything to do when he got home, since he knew he wasn't going to be catching any frogs, either.

Sister Annie, Going West

by Joe Galvan

The heat reverberates in Sister Annie's mind; it shimmers like electric air above the grey-green sea. First the train passes through the city with its tenements, its air that stinks of refuse and sewage, passing row after row of brick house with slate roofs and chimney stacks that blur one by one until they are all brown sticks against the pale smoggy blue sky of late July.

Philadelphia disappears from Sister Annie's view finally after an hour, and the world is leafy and green again; she remembers the fields of chamomile and bachelor's button of her childhood. She compares those fields in her memory to the gentle rolling fields of western Pennsylvania, where farmers leer at the train as it passes through the grades into worn hills strewn with rocks and trees. She looks back at Mother Superior reading from her prayerbook, nodding off into sleep as the Pullman car sways gently on the rails. Two white men look down on her and puff away at their cigars.

The porter, chocolate-dark and compliant, offers her lemonade.

'Where you comin' from?' the porter asks. 'Who you know out in California?'

'I'm a nun,' Sister Annie says, gently, as if she is telling a secret. To prove her point, she pulls out a rosary and fingers the crucifix with a thumb and forefinger. The porter looks at her, shakes his head and walks away.

The only thing Sister Annie has known all her life is Philadelphia. She remembers the smell of offal cooking in grease, the sound of the blacksmith cursing God and man in the streets, the acrid stench of death in the slaughterhouse, the steaming rivers of blood flowing from dead horses kicking their lives out on the cobblestones. She struggles to remember her dead mother's face, the face of her dead sister (murdered, dumped in Baltimore Harbor) and her the calloused hands of her dead brother (murdered, at Antietam). She does not know who her father was, but the stories her mother told her relate that he is kind-eyed, virile, strong, a man of tropical sensibilities and urban sophistication. Born free, you must understand. Never a slave.

The porter pushes a cart full of tea sandwiches through the aisle. A very nice man, a fellow Catholic, with an unusual gentility for 1878, pays for Sister Annie's meal.

'Are you going out West to teach Negroes and Indians to read?' he asks.

She has heard questions like these before, they are all the same, Sister Annie nods, gently, but does not look up at him.

There are many stops before the train finally accelerates out of Pennsylvania: Brooksville, Eagle, Paoli where Sister Annie and Mother Superior dine on potted roast chicken and new potatoes and a slice of chocolate cake that the sisters have baked for her. The porter delivers the newspaper, and Mother Superior squints through her pince-nez glasses to read about that den of sinners known as the US Congress. The children crowd around the windows, black and white, sticks and balls in hand, to ask why Sister Annie wears a funny hat. Sister Annie closes the shade and tries to sleep. An hour later the train is moving and everything is loud and dim. A cool breeze blows through the half-opened car window. She can smell the rain.

The next day the train is in Ohio and Indiana and the rain streaks the window. Everything is grey and wet, and for a moment it feels like a humid October afternoon. She remembers the convent in Philadelphia, the smell of starched linen and the polish of wooden veneers, the cool dark of the chapel where she prays to God. The train passes through Cincinnati, resinous and fragrant with the scent of maples, and she sees Black men and women in buckboards with fancy hats on the way to Bible study in the rain. The children run alongside the train track and yell incoherent nonsense to the nonplussed businessmen, the ladies who look away in disgust and sniff their tussy-mussies in polite contempt. Mother Superior's fingers course her rosary beads, and the two of them recite the Regina Coeli together as they pass through a city full of Italians peddling tomatoes and grapes and Greeks selling lemons and oregano, and dour-faced white women with market baskets shuffling on walkways made of planks past beautiful dark-skinned boys shoveling coal into pails. At Vincennes, Indiana, Mother Superior spies two priests step on with just suitcases that the porter struggles to pack away.

'A good sign,' she says. 'And also a bad sign.'

'Why?' Sister Annie says.

'We're almost to the West, but also amongst Mormons.'

The land abruptly flattens in Indiana and rolls out gently like a blanket spread out against heaven, Indian land. Not to the Mississippi yet, but almost there. The train groans on the rail in the heat. Sister Annie pats her brow with an embroidered handkerchief. Mother Superior splashes cool water on her face.

The conductor announces that they will be stopping for refreshment at a river.

'A godsend,' Mother Superior says, relieved.

In the plains the heat is ferocious and unforgiving. Somewhat like the people, when provoked to unjust anger. Sister Annie thinks of the men who lynched her school friend and her husband out here, for trying to buy a nag. *You don't do that out there in those parts*, a white man told Sister Annie once. She can't remember where she met him--whether it was just right after the War, when she was young, or whether it was a dying man in the hospital, or maybe a man passing through. *You don't pretend you're on equal footing with white people. I've never been prejudiced. Not one prejudiced bone in my body. If you ask me that was wrong, what they done to your friend. But you don't presume to place yourself on the square and narrow with white folks. They just won't have it.*

Here is where Sister Annie recognizes nothing. There is sky and grass, and rails. And cows. She sees an Indian dying in the street on the way down to the water hole. Mother Superior takes his temperature and gives him a bit of food, pays the doctor in the town to give him a bed to die in.

'I don't take Indians in, there's no telling what he'll do if he gets better.'

'You don't need to worry,' Mother Superior says, pressing the money into the doctor's hand.

'I'm a Lutheran, just so you know. I don't take money from no Papists.'

'It shouldn't matter who I am,' she replies. 'Just take the money.'

'Who do you think you are?' the doctor asks.

'It's not important,' Mother says. 'A good Samaritan.'

One of the priests from Vincennes, Father Dyer, rolls a cigarette out in front of the hotel where the Indian is dying. The other priest, Father Gerard, is giving the dying Indian viaticum.

'Where are you headed?'

'California. And then Washington territory.'

'Long way,' Father Dyer says, lighting the cigarette.

'You?'

'New Mexico territory,' he says. 'I'm not ready for the heat. Rather prodigious, much more so than what they lead on.'

'It's rather nice, depending on where you go in New Mexico.'

'You've been?'

'Oh yes,' Mother Superior replies sweetly. 'I taught my first classes there in Taos, after the Mexican War. I've come back east to fetch Sister Annie here to send her out to a new convent in Roseland.'

'Never have heard of it,' Father Dyer says. 'The originals of the place will be in for a surprise,' he chuckles.

The other priest comes out and shakes his head.

'We should call the undertaker.'

'How long ago did he pass?'

Father Gerard checks his pocket watch. 'Some ten minutes ago.'

The heat breaks that evening. A cool wind comes with a night fog that dissipates before the front of a violent thunderstorm.

In the hotel Sister Annie cannot stay asleep, and she watches as the lightning streaks and flashes across the sky, and she feels the thunder rumble down to her bones.

The undertaker rolls out a coffin the next morning. A few women huddle across the street to see what will happen. The priests follow the wagon, in surplice and biretta, reading the breviary. Mother Superior and Sister Annie go as far out as the burying ground, which abuts a tepid, foul-smelling stream.

They bury the Indian at three in the afternoon and pay the undertaker for a tombstone.

'Did you know his name?' they ask the undertaker.

'Indian Joe,' the undertaker replies.

Sister Annie looks at the grey sky overhead, and closes her eyes in prayer.

St Louis is a Sodom, roiling under the sun. Sister Annie sees wealthy-looking Black men in tweed suits spill from overcrowded rail cars to head over to the saloons for the three o'clock drink. She smells the scent of chili and green bell pepper and frying tripe wafting from shoddy shacks lining a muddy street.

The smokestacks of factories and foundaries belch fat columns of black smoke as far as the eye can see. The smell is sickening.

'Don't close the window,' Mother Superior says. 'We'll die of the heat if we do.'

A new conductor comes aboard and spends a long time looking at Sister Annie's ticket.

'Who told you that could sit up here, girl?'

'I did,' Mother Superior replies, firmly. 'We don't travel alone.'

'I didn't ask you,' the conductor says. 'You can't be up here. You need to get up and get on back. That's where we keep the colored folk.'

'She isn't going anywhere,' Mother Superior says.

The conductor is losing his patience and clears his voice.

'I don't think *you heard me*, ma'am. This Negro woman is forbidden on the train. Now I don't care if you're the Queen of Roumania and she's Princess Caraboo. If you don't like you, both of you should get off the train.'

The porter looks helpless as he takes their bags and sets them down gently on the platform.

'Beg your pardon, ma'am,' the porter says over and over again. 'Beg your pardon. Beg your pardon.'

'I will have to write the Archbishop.'

'I'm sorry, Mother--'

'There's nothing to be sorry about, my daughter. You did nothing wrong. Perhaps I did wrong. Maybe the Lord wanted us to ride with the other people in the back.'

'You were only doing what you thought was right,' Sister Annie says. 'Besides. I would have gotten up and gone if he wanted me to.'

'But you didn't want to,' Mother Superior says. 'And there's nothing wrong with not wanting to go to a place you don't want to go.'

Mother Superior does not sleep that night but pens a letter to the Archbishop. She hands the note to an errand boy who runs across town to the Archbishop. At seven in the morning Sister Annie is spreading jam on her toast at the hotel in St Louis when the boy comes back, with a note.

Mother Superior reads it and sits back in her chair.

'His Excellency has made protest to the railroad officials via telegraph.' She folds the note and puts it in her bag. 'They have reimbursed our tickets. We leave tomorrow evening.'

In the afternoon the nuns walk to the Cathedral alone. The men do not leer and gawk at them like they did in Vincennes. Downtown St Louis seems like a nice place to be a nun. Everyone keeps to themselves, even the Irish boys washing their horses and scrubbing the carriages, even the Black and Spanish boys corralling the horses in the carriage-house, even the German and Italian girls skipping down the block, singing to themselves and carrying armfuls of fabric and bread. The breeze picks up as they get closer to the river and for a moment Sister Annie smells linden and roses, someone's potted chicken spilling over a fire, and she hears the sounds of mothers calling in their children to eat dinner. The Cathedral in St Louis is cool and dark and still, a cold grey temple with cool pink walls inside and no one praying. Sister Annie thinks of her sister laughing in the splash of cold water from a creek they played in as a child, her mother mending a dress, the bright world of a June day mottled with green grass and little pink roses. The sunset brings a cool breeze into town and they walk back after Mass saying nothing, just as the lamps are being lit and the dust is rising in an angry, defiant little cloud that whirls itself into oblivion on the street.

'She's not going to be a problem.'

'I didn't think she was,' the station agent says.

'Please sir, we are two women religious. We don't bother anyone. I'm sure you've dealt with our ilk before. We are most happy to keep to ourselves, provided there isn't anyone to make trouble for us,' Mother Superior replies.

'Now you listen here! You best not be giving nobody any trouble, you hear me, girl?' the station agent says to Sister Annie. He has stopped looking at Mother Superior, who is shocked into silence. 'No carrying on. No loud talking. You bother one of the other patrons, I'll toss your black behind into the street where no one will render aid to you.'

The station agent slams the door to the cabin shut.

Mother Superior's frown eases. She chuckles.

'We should pray for him,' she says. 'He looks like he needs it.'

The train pulls away and Sister Annie heaves a sigh of relief. She looks out of the window. The sky is pink and purple. She watches it sink into a deep-blue against the black edge of the horizon with its smell of new-mown hay and its flickering green clouds of lightning bugs.

Four days in and they have left Missouri and Kansas, blighted with heat and struck dumb with the sound of cicadas buzzing in the locust trees, its grey rocks and its yellow ground. Kansas is nothing like she has ever seen, a flat wasteland with very little green, except for a few stark places where the trees shoot up like hands cupped to heaven as if to beg God for rain. Sister Annie drifts off to hand somewhere in-between chapters of *Introduction to the Devout Life*, she is transported in her dreams back east to the foggy dark of a Baltimore on the cusp of war, young men torching the houses of black and brown people, driving them into the street. Sister Annie sees her sister pushed through a crowd of angry boys, stripped, slapped, beaten to a pulp, pushed into Baltimore Harbor, her legs kicking in the green-black sea, her body floating amidst the whoops and hollers of the crowd, the black starless sky, the belts of waves buffeting her swollen body, the flies that hover over her lips. The nightmare is enough to jolt her just as she sees the distant mountains appear over the horizon, Mother Superior reciting the Hours quietly in her monotone.

'A nightmare,' she tells Mother Superior.

'Pray with me,' Mother Superior replies.

The landscape blurs together in a haze of pink and purple twilight, the peaks of the distant mountains growing closer, until they loom over her in Denver, in a bosom of pines that whisper in the dry south wind. She rests her eyes and in the dim light of the Pullman car she hears Mother Superior recite a litany to Our Lady of Loretto, gently, and the words wash over her like waves, *have mercy on us, have mercy on us, have mercy on us*. Carefully, she draws the quilt over her tiny body, her dark fingers slipping over the rosary beads, Mother Superior caressing her face in the dark, telling her *God bless you, daughter, first of my own flock to come to the West*. And there amid the mute granite temples of time,

Sister Annie realizes that this west is all hers now, her very own country, where the pain and the misery could be dissipated in the golden light of the west, the endless freedom of the cool fresh air, the lost and undiscovered country where the light's fingers reach into the pines to hear the touch the place where angels inscribed the burnished name of Almighty God.

The Valley

by Ben Talley

The valley appears before Elias like an open wound, festering with a fever heat between swollen hills. It seems fresh, unfamiliar to the man who has taken that route near a dozen times before. He ponders whether he has unknowingly veered from course. Easy to do so when traversing the western expanse of Texas desert unaccompanied. Yet there is something out of place here. Nature is known for her many glorious perfections, as well as her deceiving imperfections, but even so, the design of the valley appears suspiciously unnatural. The hills circle the valley with the impression of a small crater. Elias seems to stand at a steep opening down towards the valley floor, while miles directly ahead he can barely make out a pass between the hills. It seems as if he is being led into the valley's maw.

Elias' steed, Brandy, shares his suspicions, for she refuses to climb down the passage, going so far as to squeal and buck in a fit each time he so much as nudges the creature forward. Whereas Elias could have overridden his own reservations with the valley, he is willing to trust his horse's instincts. Brandy seems to be more afraid in that moment than she has ever been encountering rattlers or other more immediate dangers. Elias prepares to move them around the valley's ring, despite the significant amount of time it will add to their trek.

He tugs lightly on Brandy's reigns, attempting to steer her away from the ingress, but it proves to be too much for the already anxious mare. She enters a panic. Her hooves lose traction on the loose rocks near the hill's edge. Together they stumble forward, crashing down the jagged path. Elias is thrown from Brandy's back, a miracle that saves him from being crushed beneath her weight.

A moment later they are on the valley floor.

Part of Elias' believed miracle is that when he gets to his feet and examines his injuries he finds them to be mostly minor. Among scrapes and bruises the worst he sustains is a sprained ankle. A limp, his souvenir.

Elias' poor bronco, his trusted partner, his Brandy, is not so lucky. He hobbles over to her still body lying in the dirt. Wheezing, labored breath is all she can muster. With trepidation he gently rests his hand on her chest. She winces in pain and he pulls back. Brandy is broken. Elias can't bear it.

With one last pet and a drawing of his Colt, he eases her passing.

Following the cracking echo of his pistol a resounding silence rushes in and fills the voided space. After passing a moment to pay his respects, Elias turns to face the valley floor that stretches before him. While upon the hill's edge he could feel the heat that was trapped within the bowl lapping at his feet and his face. Now he is swimming in it.

He decides to leave his pack with Brandy, grabbing only his canteen for the long walk ahead. Any more weight will only slow him down. If he is still headed in the direction he believes himself to be, the next town will be only a day's ride ahead (three, on foot). There he can secure another horse and come back to retrieve his belongings. Assuming coyotes and the like don't drag it away with their dinner.

He only has to move forward.

What is the hesitation? The faster he walks, the sooner his current hell will be over. But the unease which gripped his horse seems to touch Elias now as well, for there is a feature of this valley that stands out to him as he faces it from the ground.

All that lay between Elias and the horizon is overgrown with cacti. Each one the size of a person. Those not so lumbering might match that of a child. He is thankful there are much fewer of that stature, for they unsettle him the most. The more he observes them in his staggered passing, the less plant-like and more statuesque they appear. He has seen this kind of cactus before, many a time in his various travels, but never in such numbers. The familiarity he has, as well, doesn't feel like that of a man recognizable with terrain, but something… different. He cannot place it. Though try as Elias might while he walks through the valley of their shadows.

The dirt is loose, closer to sand, forcing him to pick up his feet as he walks, despite his weak leg's tendency to drag itself. He

can't help but feel that he is sinking, slowly, almost impercepti-
bly, as if the ground is attempting to pull him below without his
notice. He figures this to be a delusion of heat, the same effect
that creates waves on the horizon working similarly on his
mind.

Elias hasn't made it far beneath the unforgiving sun when
the sweat his body is producing proves to be too much for his
skin. His clothes become rough with friction, chafing him to the
point he suspects he will bleed. One could posit the surrounding hills are the walls of a gargantuan forge, the way they are
cooking him.

In an attempt at the mildest of reprieves he begins to shed
his duster. He gets it past his shoulders and to his elbows when
it catches on something. Elias is able to fully remove his right
arm from the vest, but not his left. As he pulls, he can hear the
thread lightly tearing. He feels around the area of resistance and
touches something thin, like a needle, between the fabrics of
his shirt and vest. After a brief, frustrating attempt to grab hold
of the foreign object fails him, Elias elects to use the next best
thing – brute force. With a firm grip on his half-discarded coat,
he yanks.

The irreparable ripping sound that follows is accompanied by
a snap and a sharp pain unlike any he has experienced before.
Elias grips his elbow, feeling dampness thicker than sweat,
and draws his hand back to find it slick with blood. He pulls
his elbow closer for inspection and through the sleeve he sees
a deep puncture wound near as thick as a pencil, though the
sensation he felt was not penetration, but of something being
removed from his body. Confounded and honestly quite fearful
of this unknown, he searches the newly torn vest for the culprit.
What he pulls out is unmistakably a cactus needle, nearly two
inches in length. Impossible that the needle could have pierced
him recently without his knowledge, he thinks. He hadn't even
gone near one of the several surrounding cacti, but what other
explanation could there be?

He discards his vest and continues his walk. Now twice
wounded, Elias refuses to let the throbbing ache in his elbow
slow him down any more than his leg already does. The sun
eases itself down the sky towards the hills ahead of him. He
imagines it pulling the earth up over itself like a blanket for

slumber. The cooling air is a joyously welcome feeling near the end of such a tumultuous day. He is not far from the passage and believes he can make it by the sun's full setting. There he can seek shelter for the night beside some of the newly visible outcropped boulders.

Then Elias begins to notice the full extent of his hell.

The back of his left shoulder begins to itch like fire. Elias reaches up towards it with his right hand and the confident familiarity that comes with one's own body, then immediately withdraws because of a sharp sting in his palm. Fresh blood layered atop the dried from before.

He reaches back again, slowly this time, and feels around for the needle. His fingers tap around it, then grip the thing. This one is much longer, deeper he can feel once he applies pressure to its rigid body. His hand aches as he clenches a fist around the needle and tugs. His upper body jerks with it and he grimaces. It is buried deep.

Once more he grips it, ignoring his palm and his shoulder and leg, and with a deep breath he pulls with the full strength of his arm. The needle tears out of him, the sound of parting flesh deafened by his own shouting. Elias can feel hot blood spilling down his back. He inspects the needle, and beneath the thick layer of red coating its bottom half, to his horror, he sees roots. The needle is obviously no accidental transplant, but a growth. How or why in God's name, he has no idea. But he cannot deny it.

Immediately Elias becomes suspicious of his surroundings, the paranoia also taking root and growing exponentially. He scans the cacti, the sheer number of them, and notices again their striking similarities. All about his height, all with two "limbs" outstretched at shoulder length, no more, no less, and as he hobbles closer to the nearest one, he is stabbed again.

He falls to the ground, for the attack is upon his legs this time. Elias looks down at them and notices not one, but several smaller needles exuding from his legs, thigh to foot and all around. Terror rises in him as his imagination runs wild. He considers staying down, but he has a suspicion that needs to be confirmed.

Carefully, he gets to his feet. He shuffles towards the nearest cactus. It is only feet away but it may as well be a mile. Despite his efforts to keep his legs spread, the needles scrape flesh opposite them with every step. Blood pools in the heels of his boots.

When he reaches the cactus he holds his crimson palm out for balance on its shoulder, spacing his fingers around its own spikes. He stands face to face with it, quite literally. Beneath the verdant, ribbed flesh of the cactus are the indistinguishable features of a human face. The subtle curvature of cheekbones, the sunken sockets of what were once eyes, the narrow bump of a nose in the center. Clearly, it had been a man once, just as he is.

Elias turns; all the cacti seem to be watching him. He cannot be sure that they aren't.

He fears what he is to become.

Suddenly, survival instinct kicks in. Without care to how much damage he is doing to his own legs, or his abdomen now that needles are protruding from his torso and arms, he makes a run for the hills. They are not far, and he is certain he can make it before the horrific transformation is complete. He clings to the hope that he will make it out of the valley as a man, and bleed out like a man, rather than bake forever under the sun as one of those godforsaken things.

When he reaches the passage he finds it to be as steep as the one he entered the valley through. But he does not stop. He climbs, stumbles, gasps for breath, loses his footing, climbs faster. His vision blurs. He doesn't know whether it is from exhaustion or from the change, but he does not care. It does not matter. His head is pounding with the force of a hammer. He cannot stop. There is no stopping. Over and over again the needles puncture him. Elias does not stop.

He makes it to the top.

It has become near impossible to separate his thighs in step. They have fused together and are tightening on the way down to his ankles. Elias twists round for one final look at the valley. Is it for confirmation, to assure himself that it has all been real? Or is it in defiance? A look back to say, "I made it, I won"? He cannot say. Everything goes black after that.

When he awakens a stranger is by his side. The man had caught up to him on the trail, days later, miles away from Elias' dead horse. Elias is uninjured, though severely dehydrated and suffering from heat exhaustion. No scars, no sign of blood.

Elias lies in a bed provided by the Samaritan in a cabin that is unfamiliar to him. Despite not knowing where he is, he feels safe. For days he does not attempt to leave the lodging. He recovers quickly, but he dares not step outside. Instead he ponders. He pores over recent events in his mind, scrutinizing their every detail. Every sharp, piercing pain left in his memory by the cursed needles. To the stranger Elias' recounting of events seems to be the delusions of a desert drifter. Each time Elias talks of the valley, the Samaritan corrects him.

"There was no valley," he says. Elias had been found in a desert plain that stretched as far as the eye could see. No nearby hills. No cacti, not in the numbers Elias describes. Just the sun-baked hallucinations of a lost traveller.

"But you must believe me," Elias pleads.

"I do not know how the valley vanished, nor where it is now. But you must believe me. It is out there.

It is out there."

Bury me in sacred ground

by Michael Calkins

The minister held the closed bible in his lap. He hadn't bothered to open the book, but he had quoted endlessly from it. Matthew Swanson didn't mind, because it meant this was a preacher who knew the book by heart. He figured anyone who took the time memorizing it must believe at least some of what was in it. The men were sitting quietly in Matthew's cell. Matthew looked from the minister to the deputy standing by the jailhouse door pretending not to overhear. The minister was young and didn't seem to know what to do next, so Matthew broke the silence.

"Reverend, when this is over and something's got to be done with my body, I want you to make sure I'm buried in sacred ground."

The minister took a moment to answer. "If it were up to just me, Matthew, of course. But executed criminals are buried anonymously in the town field. It's not consecrated ground."

Matthew took that in and nodded. "That's what I thought, Reverend, but I still got to ask and I'll ask again. I'm paying for another man's crime and that's bad enough. I don't want to rot in unholy dirt."

"Matthew, if it was . . .," began the minister.

"I didn't kill my wife, Reverend. Of all the things I've done in my life, that's the one I would never do. Ellen was a light straight from heaven that shined on me day and night. I've been in darkness ever since I come home that day and found her body in our bed."

The Deputy made a noise that could have been clearing his throat, but Matthew knew better. He looked at the floor. "I've done plenty, alright, and I probably deserve to be punished for it all. Maybe it's waiting for me in the hereafter. God knows what I've done and He'll have His say after I'm gone. But He knows all and He's got a right. You don't know nothing."

"What don't we know, Matthew?" asked the minister. Matthew heard genuine concern in the man's voice.

"We did things to make you weep, Reverend. Things I would rather have died than let Ellen know." He looked at the minister's face. It was the face of someone who thought he could take on the worst of the world and come out clean after. Matthew had known one or two like that. But people had a way of leaving stains on each other that no amount of elbow grease and good intentions could get out. Matthew wasn't sure how much he wanted to stain this sincere, young man. But, then, he was a grown person and if he didn't yet know his limits, well, that wasn't on Matthew.

"God can forgive anything, Matthew, so long as you feel real remorse for what you've done. We are all sinners in need of being saved. And we can be, if we truly want to be. I want to help you find that forgiveness and peace before your end, Matthew. I want you to know that you can tell me anything. What don't we know?"

Matthew looked to the deputy who stood with his arms and ankles crossed. Matthew gestured for the minister to lean closer. He kept his voice low so the deputy couldn't hear and told a story in grim detail. He took his time, spared nothing, and told the whole truth as he remembered it. When he was done, he said, so the deputy could hear, "And that was only one time, Reverend. There was plenty more, if God needs to hear it."

The minister took a moment to reply, his face looking a bit pale to Matthew. "How many others, Matthew?"

Matthew shrugged. "I never kept a tally, Reverend. I suppose I could try to tell you about all of them that I remember and you could count for yourself. We never talked about what we done after we done it. We just moved on and never went back. That was one of the rules."

"You say 'we', Matthew. Who were the others?"

"Not others, Reverend. Just him and me. It was only ever him and me. He made the rules and they worked good, kept us out of trouble. No lawman ever even talked to us and we never had a reason to talk to them. The only time I ever talked to the law was when I came in to town to tell the sheriff that someone had killed Ellen. You see how that worked out." The deputy chuckled.

"Who was he, Matthew? It might do you good to let someone know. It might go to your account if he was brought to justice."

"I can't do that, Reverend. His sins ain't mine to confess." When Matthew had left his friend, he had had no hard feelings toward him. It was just time to go. Matthew had been drinking too much and feeling bad about what they were doing, so he had just packed up one night and rode quietly away from camp. If he had wanted some justice to go to his account, he thought, he could have put a bullet in his sleeping friend that night. What he had wanted, though, was some peace, which he had had when he found Ellen.

The minister was about to say something when the door to the jailhouse opened and two armed men walked in. The sheriff exchanged glances with the deputy as he walked over to the cells. "Preacher, I don't like to interfere with someone doing the Lord's work, but we are nearing the appointed time." The minister seemed unsure what to do.

Matthew said, "Reverend, there's the Lord's work and there's the government's. I think the Lord is going to have to wait His turn."

The minister put his hand on Matthew's. "I'll be with you the whole time, Matthew, if you'd like me to be."

Matthew nodded. "For what little good it'll do me, Reverend, you go right ahead." The minister stood and stepped to the door of the cell. At a gesture from the sheriff, the deputy came forward with the keys and opened the door to let out the minister. Then the sheriff instructed Matthew to turn around and put his hands behind his back. Soon enough his arms were shackled and he was standing outside the cell. The sheriff went to his desk and took some papers from a drawer.

"I reckon we're ready," said the sheriff. He opened the jailhouse door, stood there for a moment, then gestured for the others to follow him out. When they were outside, the sheriff led the way, then came Matthew, who was flanked by the deputy and the other man. The minister followed.

The scaffold, which Matthew had heard them building yesterday, was nearly surrounded by people. Children were running around or sitting on their father's shoulders. Everyone seemed done up in their Sunday best. Some women twirled parasols and picnic baskets had been set on the ground here and there. There was nothing like a hanging to get a town's attention, Matthew knew.

The group of men had paused just outside the jailhouse, but the sheriff said, "Alright," and they started toward the scaffold. Some in the crowd had caught sight of them and were pointing them out to the others. Though Matthew had not been a regular in town, he recognized many of the people. People who had referred to him as, "that man the Bascom girl married". He had been proud to be that man. That was a man who had tried to make something of his life, small though it was.

A shaggy dog jumped onto the scaffold. Matthew watched it, full of life, run around on the platform. Some in the crowd laughed until the sheriff and the deputy chased it away. When the scaffold was clear, the sheriff led the men onto it. The deputy pushed Matthew into place beneath the noose, but left the rope hanging free. Matthew wanted a drink. He felt a little ashamed for wanting one, because he had been weak before and it had cost him so much. But a man who was facing his last moments, he figured, maybe had a right to be weak.

He hadn't had a right to be weak that day he had been in the city to sell his harvest. Prices had been good. He had managed a good crop, so he had been flush with cash. It had been more money than he had seen since the old days when they would, mostly, just take it. But he had earned this money with a strong back and the love of a good woman. Some of the other farmers there, men he hadn't known, had talked him into celebrating with them. He'd been weak to agree.

The sheriff cleared his throat and began to read from the papers he had brought. There was Latin and legal-talk nobody understood, but there was no mistaking the phrases "guilty of murder" and "hanged by the neck until dead". There was hollering and insults from the crowd. Matthew looked straight ahead, over the people, not one of whom had really cared about "that Bascom girl" until she was gone. Not like Matthew had.

But he had been weak and had gone to the saloon with the

farmers. For a time he had kept his promises to Ellen. But a pretty, young woman with red cheeks, big, brown eyes, and thick, black hair piled on her head, had put a hand on his shoulder. She had introduced herself and acted like she was interested in him. She had been prettier than most of the whores Matthew had ever seen. With his friend not there to enforce the rules and Ellen back home and out of sight, Matthew had been weak.

First, he had started drinking and had broken that promise to Ellen. When he had been drunk enough, he had gone upstairs with the woman, had paid her money, and had broken his marriage vows. When they had finished, Matthew had gone back to the bar. One of the farmers had seen him come down and had come over to slap him on the back and offer to buy him a drink. Matthew had nodded. When he had finished the drink, Matthew had left the saloon for his wagon and had headed straight out of town.

The sheriff asked Matthew if he had any last words to say. Matthew paused a moment, then said he did. The crowd became hushed. He didn't really know what he was going to say. He looked to the minister. "Before we came out here, I was talking to the Reverend. I told him I wanted him to make sure I was buried in sacred ground." This caused a stir in the crowd. "I know that ain't likely. Right or wrong, you all will decide what happens. I've been a bad man. I can't deny that. But I've tried to be a good man, too. And, maybe, that ought to count for something.

"I loved Ellen more than anything. I know I was a disappointment to her sometimes. But ain't we all, sometimes, to somebody? I hope I'll see her again so I can ask her forgiveness for those disappointments. But I won't have to ask forgiveness for her death, because I did not do that. For that my conscience is clean." More insults came from the crowd.

On his way back home, drunk though he had already been, Matthew had stopped the wagon to climb in the back and grab a bottle of whiskey he had stashed there. It had been his intention never to drink it, but only to have it there as a reminder. He had climbed back into the seat as he had pulled out the cork with his teeth. The bottle had become half empty by the time he had arrived home after midnight.

The house had been dark and he had sat in the wagon for a long while deciding what to do. Finally, he had decided just to go in. If she woke and saw that he was drunk, he would confess everything. Throw himself on her mercy. He had opened the door as quietly as he could. He had crawled into bed next to her, all of his clothes still on. He had reached for her and his hand had felt an unexpected wetness.

He had stumbled from the bed and did his drunken best to light a lamp. He had known, though, what he would find in the light. He had had too much experience of it. Despite that, he had crawled back into bed, had held her, soaking his shirt red. Hours later he had gone to town, still drunk, to talk to the sheriff.

The deputy put the noose around Matthew's neck and whispered a last insult. Matthew didn't really hear it. In his mind he heard the sheriff tell him he was under arrest. He heard the jury foreman say that they had found him guilty. He heard himself make promises to Ellen. He figured now that Satan must have been laughing when Matthew made those promises. He was no good and never would be, try as he might. Only it didn't seem fair that anyone else had to pay for his weakness.

Ellen was buried in the churchyard. They had never let him visit the grave. They would never bury him next to her. Maybe he should never have tried to be better, he thought. He heard the creak of the trapdoor lever moving. And then, like on that miserable,drunken night, the world fell out from under Matthew Swanson.

Horse People

by Geoff Wallin

The old man, tired, hungry, sunburned, and sore, pushed himself through the saloon doors, his joints creaking louder than the creaky old hinges. Inside the bar, his feet fell on even creakier floorboards, and he heard the wobbly strains of a honky-tonk piano, even creakier still. He had a headache, and he longed for quiet.

He breathed the dusty air and hacked a creaky cough that rattled through his chest like a dried out snake skin. He paused, inhaled long through his nose, and stopped cold. Suddenly he felt uncomfortable. The bar was full of horse people.

Well, he thought, crossing his arms over his puffed up chest and spreading his legs wide, *now it's full of me.*

A clock bell tolled the bottom of the hour.

The old man walked slowly over to an empty bar stool and sat down, far enough from the horse people to be alone, close enough to seem lonely. He was bitter, and he wanted what was owed him.

These were horse people, all right. He could smell the hay. He could smell it all over them. Some of it didn't smell like hay, but it was. It had just passed through a horse once, that's all. What you had to pass through to become a horse person, he didn't want to know.

He sniffed the air again. These horse people smelled okay, for horse people. It was the hay. Good, fresh hay. Good hay meant good horses, and good horses meant good horse people. Bad hay was just another kind of neglect, and neglect was just another kind of poison.

But these horse people, they smelled like the good kind of horse people, the kind of horse people who took care of their horses, brushed them and braided their manes, fed them good hay. Good horse people loved their horses; they just neglected everything else in their lives. Neglected it til it withered and died.

In the end, horse people were horse people. He had no friends in horse people, and he took comfort in the knowledge that they were more afraid of him than he was of them. He could smell the fear, right along with the hay. But my, that was some fine smelling hay. Fresh cut timothy. Or was it alfalfa?

"Hey," said the bartender, "you gonna order somethin'?"

The old man looked hard at the bartender. "Yeah. I'll have me a horse steak, rare." The old man saw the horse people overhear him, and he heard the piano stop playing. The room was silent.

The bartender barely moved. "Sorry mister, we can't cook it rare."

"Yeah?" said the old man, "How's that?"

"Well, in these parts, horses are awful common." The horse people laughed quietly.

"Is that so?" said the old man with cold sarcasm.

"I'm afraid it is."

The old man was unfazed. "In that case, I suppose I'll have it well done."

The bartender frowned slowly. "Sorry, mister. The only thing 'round here that's well done is the water." The laughter was louder now, and one of the horse people, a middle aged man, stood up and started walking slowly over.

The old man grew angry. "Then I suppose I'll just have to have it cooked medium," he said through gritted teeth.

"Mister," said the bartender, "this ain't no wishin' well, and it ain't no blarney stone, neither, and I ain't gonna read your mind if'n you ain't even gonna read the menu." The horse man was close now, and the stink filled the old man's face, but still he couldn't make out the hay. Was that timothy, or alfalfa?

"Timothy!" came a woman's voice, "where're you goin'?"

"It's all right, Winnie, don't you worry none," said the horse man, and he turned to the bartender, "it's all right, Ed, this gentleman ain't from here and don't know no better." He smiled warmly at the old man, tried to make him feel at ease. "My name's Timothy, and this here's my place, and I apologize on behalf of my friend and bartender, Ed, here. Ed ain't used to strangers. And around here, well, you start orderin' dinner the way you did just now, sooner or later you're bound to offend somebody. Just so happened that it happened sooner than later, that's all. Might be you're lucky that way."

"It's all right," said the old man, feigning warmth, and he turned to the bartender. "Don't worry about it, Ed."

"That's Mister Ed to you, fella," said Ed, "but I reckon I owe you an apology anyhow, on account of the jokes. I'm right sorry about that. I didn't mean no disrespect; it's just that, well, we don't serve no horse meat 'round here. We don't serve no meat of no kind. This here's a vegetarian restaurant."

"That's right," said Timothy.

The old man chuckled. He was wasting his time. He was hungry, but he wasn't that hungry. Nevertheless he was angry, and vegetarian restaurant or not, he had a bone to pick. But he had to bide his time. "Well," he said, "what do you recommend?"

Ed spoke up. "Let's see, we just got us a mess of the freshest sprouts this side of the Ogallala River, sweeter than a July cantaloupe and springier than the month of May."

"Alfalfa?" asked the old man.

"Timothy," said Winnie, "why don't you invite him to come on over and join us?"

"Well?" a hopeful Timothy said to the old man, "what do you say?"

The old man grew tense with anticipation. He had them right where he wanted them, but he couldn't let on. "Golly, I, I just don't know."

"You go on," said Ed. "Have yerself a seat over there and take a gander at the menu, and I'll bring you a glass of water, well done."

The old man shifted ominously on his stool, his elbow crooked, his back sore, his neck hot with sunburn, his head throbbing, his mouth dry, his stomach growling, his heart beaten. The moment was his, but he had to play it slow. He had to play it slow and mean.

"Come on," said Timothy with a friendly smile and a welcoming gesture. "We'll find somethin' to satisfy, sure enough."

The old man stayed in his seat. "I'm much obliged, I really am, and I thank you and I thank you kindly," he said softly. "But the fact is that I simply can't abide by horse folk. Please don't take it personal. I'm sure you're all fine people, and I'm not saying I'm any different, no sir. I've mucked out a stall or two myself, let me tell you, and I've bucked my share of hay. I've done my time in a horse barn, and let's just say I've been kicked. So no, I won't be joining you. And besides, I'll need to get some real food in me if'n I'm a gonna make it through the night. I don't reckon I'd last long without meat. Horse meat, preferably."

Timothy looked the old man over and nodded slowly. "Well, sir," he began, a note of disappointment in his voice, "I reckon I know when to leave well enough alone, but I can't say as I'm not real sorry to hear all that, and I hope you'll come 'round to a change of heart. And even though Ed told you this ain't no wishin' well, we'll be wishin' you well, anyhow." He struggled to smile, more defensive now.

"Much obliged," said the old man, and he turned back to the bar. He sat coiled, ready to strike, as taut as an old lesson. He struck. "But you know what they say."

Timothy stood wary. "What's that?

The old man swallowed hard and looked Timothy cold in the eye. "You can't spell Lipizzaner without pizza."

Timothy's brow furrowed and his cheeks fell. He scratched his head. "Now what the heck do ya mean by that?"

The old man stood up and raised his voice a notch. "What I mean is this. A little horse fat would grease up them hinges right good, a couple of horse hides would muffle them floorboards real nice, and a big juicy horse steak would keep that piano player quiet for a couple more chimes of that clock bell. And let me remind you that I've got a hankerin' for some horse meat myself, a hankerin' that's got to be satisfied, one way or another. That's what I mean by that."

Timothy started for him and stopped himself, fists clenched by his sides. "Now you wait just a minute there, mister." He struggled to control himself. "You wait just a goll-dern minute and listen here. Them hinges tell me when somebody comes through them doors, and them floorboards tell me how far they get. As for the piano player, she tells me that we live in a beautiful world that's full of hope and joy and all kinds of goodness, and I'd sooner drag you clear on to hell than tell my youngest girl-child she can't practice when and where she pleases, especially with a recital comin' up.

"Now, you done gone and offended us once or twice already, talkin' that way, and we done gone and let it go, seein' as how you come from far off. But I believe I done made it clear just how things is around here, and I believe you done seen the line I drew, and I believe you done crossed that line with intent. I believe you done intentionally tried to rile me up, and I can't say as I appreciate it. But it ain't in my or my family's interest to enter into a quarrel with you, and I don't reckon I will. We won't have none of that here." He relaxed just enough to show the old man he was serious, but he stayed on his guard, his eyes never leaving eyes that never left his. But the old man's eyes, and his mouth, were silent.

Timothy continued. "Mister, I don't know what you got against horses, but it ain't no concern of mine. That's your burden, and it's clearly a ponderous one, and for that I pity you." The edges of his voice broke under the weight of his sadness. "But it ain't my business, and I reckon your business waits elsewhere, if'n you got any business aside from building maintenance services, of which I am not in need at this time. So I reckon you'd best be gettin' on. This here's a farmin' community. We pick vegetables. You'll see better someplace else, if'n you're lookin' to pick a fight."

The old man, defeated, took a slow, creaky step back. He nodded to Timothy, surrendered deferential glances to Ed and to the horse people, and he turned away. He didn't say a word, didn't make a sign, just passed back through those creaky swinging doors, off into the dusty street, a blown out tumbleweed, dried up and lost, rolling as it goes where the wind goes to die, where the words aren't so many, and the memories not

so keen, where the silence tells a truth lit soft by northern lights,
and the dark, half-empty valleys shelter mystery and lies.

A Gathering of Tinies

by Fred White

It was the Wheatland Tiny (now self-designated Tiny-1) who'd thought it would be a nifty idea to locate all the large cowboys (literal cowboys as well as cowboys-at-heart) nicknamed "Tiny" not just in Wyoming, but all across the West, and invite them to his Wheatland ranch for a celebration. A celebration of what, you ask? Hell, cowboys don't need a reason to celebrate; but as Tiny-1 explained to each of the eight cowboys he contacted, it's to celebrate ourselves for being so big that people want to nickname us the opposite of what we are, and get a good laugh out of it. High time we inject some sorely needed good-natured American humor—cowboy style—into the world.

A few days later, the eight Tinies met at Tiny-1's ranch for a planning session.

"Folks don't care much about cowboys anymore, Tiny," groused Tiny-2, a fellow cattle rancher from nearby Torrington. "Certainly not cow-hulks like us."

"Folks care about cowboys out in these parts," said Tiny-3 from Billings, Montana. Tiny-4 added, "That also goes for all the Western and Southwestern states, plus the Dakotas, Nebraska and Kansas. Not counting Californey of course, with all them degenerates in La-La Land."

"There's lotsa cowboys in Northern Cal, and the Central Valley, Tiny; you won't find no degenerates in Redding, I can tell you."

"Lemmee tell you somethin' about us cow-hulks," interjected Tiny-5 from Ogden, Utah. "The bigger we are, the better. Folks cain't overlook us when we take up more space'n' a pregnant sow."

Tiny-1 stood up. "Let's talk about grub for the gathering—and beer!"

"I'll supply the beer kegs," said Tiny-6, a rodeo manager from Casper.

"Maybe we can each share stories about what it was like growing up bear-sized!" suggested Tiny-7, a veterinarian and former
cowboy from Dwyer.

"We should make that the highlight of the gathering, said
Tiny-8, a cowboy poet and former trucker who now taught a
course in Western folklore at UW Laramie. "It would let the
world know that we're not just a bunch of oversized shit-kicking
rednecks."

"Hey, I'm proud of being a shit-kicking redneck." Tiny-4 said.

The eight Tinies decided to hold their Great Western Tiny
Shindig in mid-May. Tiny-6 would prepare publicity releases;
Tiny-7 would create poster art depicting Tinies circumscrib-
ing the Wyoming State logo of a rodeo rider, one hand on his
saddle, the other waving his hat.

*

Two weeks later . . .

"I still cain't figure out what in perdition is the point of such
a foolhardy gathering," Tiny-2 wanted to know. "Is it to stereo-
type us even more than we've already been?"

"Yeah," agreed Tiny-3. "They all like to think of us as back-
woods bruisers, all brawn, no brains."

"My brawn *is* my brains," proclaimed Tiny-6 proffering his
beer bottle.

To which Tiny-8 replied: "The point is, we don't have to be ac-
countable to nobody. Anyone who don't approve of us, well, you
know where they can shove their heads."

As it turned out on that fine Saturday afternoon in early May,
close to a hundred Tinies (not all of them "tiny" in the original
eight Tinies' sense of the word, but that was not held against
them) showed up at Tiny-1's Wheatland ranch—many of them
from other states who'd gotten word of the strange request:
cowboy farmers from Idaho, Montana, Texas, and Oklahoma;
cowboy business execs from Utah, cowboy casino workers from
Nevada—huge men, young and old—and several voluptuous
cow gals! The press had gotten word of the event and showed up
with their TV equipment.

Did the hundred Tinies merely lounge around swilling beer and gnawing on beef jerky? No. Did they hold tractor-pulling contests? No. Did they arm-wrestle? Well, some did. But mostly they spun campfire-style yarns and recited poetry. In fact, quite a few of them were bona fide cowboy poets! Some of the poems they turned into songs and sang through the evening, the aroma of barbecued venison wafting over the ranch. What did they sing about? Why, songs about herding cattle and riding bucking broncos; songs about wind-swept mesas; songs of saddling up at dawn; songs celebrating the American frontier that still lived on in their oversized cowboy hearts.

No Eulogies

by Michael Santiago

"Ava, grab Morgan and get down!" a disgruntled, bearded outlaw yelled within a desolate lodge.

The blistering sound of bullets rattled that very lodge that was isolated and nestled alongside the

Appalachian mountains. Each devastating round tore the lodge asunder as the sound of a child crying could be heard from within.

Ava made haste to grab Morgan, their only child, but saw her husband riddled with bullets as he clawed his way to find his holster. Slithering across the floor leaving a trail of blood, he grabbed his gun with trembling hands. He frantically placed six rounds in the cylinder and slammed it shut. His mind was racing as fast as his heart, and he knew that it was time to own up for his sins.

"Now listen here, Ava, take the boy to the cellar, lock it shut, and don't you come out until its dead silent.

Don't make a peep no matter what happens..." he muttered as he began to cough up blood while gripping his wife's hand.

"Carson... baby... how did it come to this?" Ava cried.

"Dammit, Ava, get into the cellar now. I'm begging you, love." He replied as a tear trembled down his eye.

Just outside, four men on horseback offered a cold, solemn stare at the lodge.

"Now we're here for Carson. We have no quarrel with anyone else that may be dwelling about inside.

Give us the two-timing bastard and we'll let anyone lingering survive past sundown," declared a

displeased and clean shaven bandit.

"Is that you... Abraham?" muttered Carson.

"Why yes it is, Carson. You ran off with our fair share of the haul, yet you decided to stir up some chaos among your brothers. You did have that grand dream of retiring with your wife... Ava... is that right? And what about that young pup, Morgan? Are they in there too? You really think you're gonna enjoy them earnings? Boy, do you hear me? Do you think you can just turn your back on your own brothers after we took all that money from Uncle Sam?" stated Abraham with vexed look.

"You always did have a knack for running your gums, Abraham," replied Carson.

"I've had enough of this pretend cow poke. Chester, Jeremiah, Obadiah... lets end this bastard here now.

What do you say, boys?" Abraham confessed.

"Oh boss, I've been waiting for this here day to come for a while now," confirmed Jeremiah.

"Never thought much of this rat anyways," Chester followed.

"Now, now listen here Abraham. Do you feel this is absolutely necessary? And what of his family?" Obadiah argued.

"Are you giving me lip, Obadiah? You always did have a hard on for ole Carson didn't ya? Now what I say goes. And on this very day, Carson will be laid to rest. All of you dismount, and lets get this over with. No survivors today," shouted Abraham.

Chester, Jeremiah, and Abraham dismounted their steeds as Obadiah grew hesitant about what would transpire. He looked at his brothers as if he were watching a pack of wolves hunt a family of deer.

"Chester, Jeremiah, get that damn door down. And Obadiah, get your ass over here and help out. Unless, you intend on joining Carson today," Abraham declared.

Obadiah followed suite and approached the lodge, but it didn't sit well with him. After all, he's the one that convinced Carson to get on board with the heist due to a childhood promise he made to him.

When Carson was 8-years-old, his mother ran off with another man who had accrued much more money than his father.

Only a year after, his father perished from typhoid fever, which left him an orphan.

Obadiah, only three years older, lived next door with his family, and convinced his father to take Carson in. The two grew close in a relatively short period, and it was Obadiah's promise that he would help Carson achieve all the wealth he could ever have so that he could one day have his own family. This gave the young Carson a plethora of hope.

"Abraham, I implore you to reconsider this. You said you'd spare anyone else lingering about," pleaded Obadiah.

"The damn decisions made. Now shut the hell up. There ain't no turning back now. He made a decision and threw his own life away." Abraham spoke with resentment.

Inside the lodge, Carson stood up, trembling, and spewing blood all over the floor. Clenching his chest, he knew his time was near. He reached for a photo of his wife on the table next to the fireplace, and said, "You were the one who took a gamble on me, and I loved you dearly for it. My beloved, Ava, I'm sorry this road took us here. In this life or the next, I will hold every memory of you dear. You were my godsend, and gave us a miracle. I'll miss you both."

"Ava, I love you, honey. Look after our boy, and tell him his father loved him more than anything this damn cash could ever buy," stated Carson.

A loud thud could be heard behind Carson. Abraham walked without a word past Chester and Jeremiah, who both managed to get the door down. He reached for his gun, pulled it out, and fired several rounds into Carson's chest. Chester collapsed on the cellar doors with his wife's picture in hand. His breathe slowed, and his words became garbled.

"What's this, Carson?" Abraham spoke inquisitively as he snatched the photo from his twitching hand.

"Boys, now ain't his wife a beaut? Where's this little she devil now?" Abraham spoke in a callous and secheming tone.

"I gave... you... all my... best," Carson uttered with his last breathe.

"Now did you?" Abraham spoke as he lifted his gun.

The resounding sound of a gun shot rattled and echoed throughout the woods nearby. Ava, just below the floorboards, was privy to what had occurred. She hugged Morgan and began weeping uncontrollably.

Her own grief was the catalyst for what happened next.

"Woooo, can you hear that? I think I hear a damsel in distress feeling sorrow for her late husband. I wonder where she is. Ava... Ava... it's OK dear. There ain't nothing to cry for no more. You can blame all this on Carson, the man who preached of loyalty, yet had none in his last moments. Don't you see this clearly? He betrayed his own brothers, you, and that son of yours. You should be grateful we put such a hypocrite out his own misery," Abraham snickered as he slowly crept towards the cellar doors.

Without notice, Abraham opened those very doors exposing a hollow and mournful Ava. "Ah, is that the boy? He bears an uncanny resemblance to his father," he said as he pointed at Carson's corpse.

"Boys, grab Carson's whore out of there! And Obadiah, get the child," shouted Abraham.

Chester and Jeremiah reached in to yank Ava out as she began shaking compulsively. "Since you two have expressed such loyalty unlike our dearly departed brother, I'm going to treat you to something special. You two can have your way with her, but at least take it upstairs. We are decent folk after all," proclaimed Abraham as he began laughing hysterically.

"Oh, and you, Obadiah, you're welcome to the boy as well. Just take it outside, would ya?" Abraham mockingly suggested.

Obadiah took Morgan and shoveled him outside with haste. He tossed him onto the back of his steed and whispered "Stay here. Your daddy was a brother to me, which therefore makes your momma my sister.

As for me, I'm just an educated bandit. It war your poppa who had the big dreams. It should've been me in his place."

Obadiah made his way back towards the lodge, but with both

of his revolvers in hand. As he made his way over the torn down door, he said "Abraham, it wasn't my intention, but now I have to reconsider this travesty. I will join Carson, my only brother, today, if I must."

Abraham turned around with an obtuse smile plastered across his face and shouted "Then lets get on it with, hero." As Abraham raised his arm to fire, Obadiah blastcd several holes into his chest before his body plummeted to the floor.

"Hey boss, what's going on down there? Ain't the poor bastard dead enough?" Chester yelled from the second floor as Ava could be heard screaming.

"Chester, Carson just rose from the dead and took out Abraham. Y'all boys better come down here quick. Carson won't be a problem no more, but we got to sort out what's just happened to dear old Abraham," Obadiah replied as an effort to lure the other two.

"God damn, just when we were about to have our fix the boss has to go ahead and get croaked by a dead man. This doesn't smell right, Chester. We saw the boss put a bullet right into Carson's head. I think you better go check on Abraham," Jeremiah spoke with a confused stare.

"Alright, but don't you get greedy and keep her all to yourself. I need to get my fix before sundown,"

Chester declared as he walked out of the bedroom.

"Oh hush, I'm gonna have my way with this wag-tail now. Now vamoose," Jeremiah spoke fervently as he began to rip off Ava's clothes.

Chester made his way down the staircase with his pistol in hand, and his eyes fixated on the lifeless void that was now Abraham's final resting place. He uprooted his gaze to see Obadiah breathing heavily with a white-eyed stare in return. "What the hell is this, Obadiah? Why are you holding your gun like that?"

Chester reverberated with an abstract tone.

No hesitation was offered for what happened next. Obadiah placed a bullet square between Chester's eyes as he fell to the ground next to Abraham. "You up there, Jeremiah, I need to have a word with you," he bellowed at the top of his lungs.

As he made his way upstairs, he could hear the sound of Ava crying endlessly. Every step he took matched his heartbeat, and as he approached the door, he wondered. He wondered about how everything had to come to this, and if intrinsic values such as loyalty held any real place in this world anymore. As if the west no longer had a place for men like Obadiah and Carson. He recalled a conversation he had with Carson shortly after his parents died.

"Carson... Carson... get your hide over here and take a gander at this," young Obadiah spoke while holding a 15th century Spanish Dollar up in the air.

"Obadiah, what ya holding?" an inquisitive and youthful Carson replied.

"This here is the key to our future, brother. We're going to be rich as soon as we can get you to ride a horse properly," he laughed with a candid look. "But what makes us brothers, is that when your poppa died, I decided I'd look after you. Do you know what that's called, Carson? Loyalty. And brothers need to be loyal to one another. So I promise you, I'll make sure you have more riches then you could ever possibly dream. And we'll get there together, do you understand?" he spoke with absolute certainty.

"Loyalty. Like no matter what we'll look after each other?" Carson responded with a timid curiosity.

"Yes, that's what that means, Carson," Obadiah spoke with confidence.

"Huh, loyalty," he said to himself as he opened the door to see Jeremiah having his way with Ava.

"Jeremiah, get off her. You know this ain't right. We were brothers loyal to a cause, our cause," Obadiah proclaimed with utter intensity.

Jeremiah retreated from his position to grab his gun while he buckled up his pants. He snatched Ava off the bed and placed the barrel against her temple and insisted that Obadiah back down.

"Now, Oby, I can appreciate your dedication and fervency to this idea of loyalty, but you should've had that talk with Carson before he put us here in the first place," Jeremiah commented with the pressure of the gun increasing against Ava's temple.

"Let her go, Jeremiah. Do you want to make poor ole Morgan an orphan?" Obadiah yelled back.

"That don't matter no more. Carson made his choice, and you made yours," Jeremiah spoke softly as he pulled the trigger. He began to laugh as manically as Abraham did when after he murdered Carson in cold blood, and then suddenly shifted his focus onto Obadiah through the barrel of his gun.

They began to fire erratically at each other, and as they both collapsed, Obadiah spoke, "Carson, the only thing that I ever gave a damn about was loyalty. But that doesn't matter, I let you down brother. Now, I'll be seeing you and Ava real soon," muttered a dying Obadiah.

Outside, Morgan dismounted Obadiah's steed to make his way towards the bloodbath that just ensued. He saw the lifeless body of his father strewn across the floor, and just a few inches away, the cadavers of Chester and Abraham blocked the staircase. His eyes grew heavy with tears, and he began to let his tears manifest through what he was witnessing.

As he made his way to parents room, he could only hear the sound of the wind whistling through the bullet holes. He pushed open the bedroom door and saw his mother, Jeremiah, and Obadiah on the floor.

In a moment, his entire life was forever altered by the different notions of loyalty. He knew his father was loyal to his family, but Abraham was loyal to himself, and Obadiah was loyal to a promise that bound him to Carson.

Morgan fell to his knees, placed his hands on his eyes, and he let out a horrifying scream.

HEL
@akrea

The Red Bandana

by Hannah Collins

It was the first day this town had seen a woman marshal. On my way into town all the locals were givin' me nasty looks, but it wasn't gonna despair me. I was there to do a job and that's what I was gonna do. I didn't have time for those chuckleheads. I know I'm good at catchin' outlaws; that's how I became the first woman marshal back in Petersburg. I came to Oaks Ridge to help the local sheriff and if they tried to give me trouble, they had another thing comin'.

All I knew about the case I was workin' was that there was a gang of men that had been thievin' cattle. Now, the reason they called me wasn't because I'm a cattle expert but because they were thinkin' this might lead us to the Phantom Riders. I'd been workin' their case for months and hadn't been able to pin them down. I'd only seen them in the flesh once. Back in Scottsdale I saw the eyes of the Devil himself. He was wearin' a bandana across his face and had eyes as black as coal. From that point on I knew I had to be the one to bring those evil men down.

Now, this gang, well they're faster than a slicked up pig on a mudslide. They leave town so fast that nearly nobody sees them. That's why they're named the Phantom Riders. All we knew was that they wear a red skull on their coats and that every town they've gone through they leave a red trail behind them. I've been cleanin' up that trail without no leads. Until now. I'm crossin' every finger and toe I got that I finally catch those bastards.

I talked to the local sheriff and after a few scoffs he gave me all the details I needed. When the rancher saw his cows gettin' thieved, he saw a red skull on the thieves' coats. That sure seems like a dumb mistake to make for a gang of killers who have made it through six towns without being caught. The sheriff thinks they have a base set up in the hills behind the town.

"Evelyn, we gotta take it slow here," the sheriff told me.

I disagreed. We needed to ambush them. I knew how they worked and yet this coot wasn't believin' me. Why did you ask for my help if you ain't gonna use it?

"Sheriff, I've been followin' this gang for months. I know how they operate. We need to act fast."

After some struggle I finally got the sheriff to agree to my plan. I told him to get all his men, get all the gear and get as much whiskey as he can find. 'Cause we were gonna be celebratin'.

The sheriff, his men, and I headed up to the Ashwood Hills on our horses. We tied them up to some trees 'bout 100 yards from where the Phantom Riders were last seen. I saw a bit of smoke in the sky and told the sheriff to move in but don't get seen. We had to be sneaky to ambush these fools. We were about to get to their camp when a shot was fired. We quickly fell back behind some logs.

More bullets flew by my head while I was thinkin' up a plan. "We gotta go for it." I looked out above the log and whipped out my pistol. A couple of my shots landed and I heard yowls. I saw five more men and their leader. He was wearin' the same bandana as I had remembered. As red as the blood he was about to bleed. Right after the sheriff and his men took some shots, it was finally over. The whole gang was on the ground bleedin'. I walked up to the leader and tore off that goddamned bandana. I wanted to see his face before I shot him dead. What I saw shook me straight outta my boots. Starin' back at me was my own brother. I took a step back.

"What? John? Is…is that you?" Those were the only words that could come out of my mouth.

"Hey sis. Long time no see."

I hadn't seen my brother in about a decade. I had always wondered where he ran off too after our Pa died. I had never thought he'd be in a gang killin' innocent folks.

"Why? Why are you doin' this? I've been followin' you for months now, from town to town. Seein' the deaths stack up. I can't believe this." I said.

"Well, believe it, Ev. After Pa died I didn't care about my life or anyone else's." John looked down at his feet, almost shameful. "Sis, I'm tired. I'm tired of runnin' and I'm tired of hidin'. I think I'm finally ready to call it quits. When I saw you in Scottsdale I knew what you were up to. It made me rethink a lot of my life decisions." John chuckled. "So go ahead sis. I know why you're here. Get it over with."

A million thoughts ran through my head. I can't shoot my own flesh and blood. But he's killed so many poor folks. Then, out of nowhere, a shot rang through my ears. I saw the life in my brother's eyes disappear. I turned around and saw the sheriff.

"You was hesitatin.'"

"He was my brother you son of a bitch!" I screamed at him.

"I don't care if it was your brother or not. This is why we can't have lady cops. You're all too damned emotional." The sheriff said to me.

I walked towards him and punched him in the face. "Fuck you." I walked back to John and fell to my knees. "You bastard. I didn't want you dead." I pulled the bottle of whisky out from my bag and took a swig. Even though I wasn't celebratin', I'd be drinkin' anyway.

Hiram Mitchell

by Michael Calkins

Not being one to like crowds much, Hiram Mitchell had stopped his horse down the street, far enough to be away from the people and close enough to see the scaffold. He checked his watch and found it was 11:40, which was a little early to his taste since they weren't meant to hang the prisoner until noon. But so long as no one wanted to talk to him or take the time to be friendly, Hiram Mitchell was satisfied to sit in his saddle and wait.

A fly took up residence around the right ear of his horse and its buzzing and bothering set the horse to twitching its ear. When the fly wouldn't go away and the horse wouldn't stop twitching, Hiram Mitchell snatched at the insect and caught it in his fist. The horse's ear became still and Hiram Mitchell knew he had made the right choice. He crushed the fly in his fist then opened his hand and flicked the corpse off his glove. So long as no one came by to bother him . . . .

Hiram Mitchell had never been in this town, though he had been around it. When he had heard that his old friend, Matthew Swanson, had been arrested for murdering his own wife, Hiram Mitchell had wanted to keep an eye on the proceedings from a distance. So he had taken a room in a boarding house run by an old woman. From there he had read the papers and kept an ear open for any gossip from the townsfolk. But now that they were going to hang his old friend, Hiram Mitchell decided it would be worth coming in so he could know with his own eyes that Matthew was dead. It was a shame, really. Matthew had been the best friend Hiram Mitchell had ever had. The only friend, if truth be told. But life was full of unpleasant necessities and watching an old friend hang turned out to be one of them.

The crowd around the scaffold was thickening, but was still safely far from him. There was nothing in Hiram Mitchell's experience that could draw folks out like a hanging, unless it was fireworks. People were dressed in their Sunday best and some were carrying picnic baskets, looking to make a day of it, apparently. Hiram Calkins reached into his saddle bag and pulled out a handkerchief that was wrapped around some vanilla cake the old woman at the boarding house had given him. She told folks she had bought the house with money her husband had left her when he died. But Hiram Mitchell knew an old whore when he saw one. She must have done alright for herself, though, to afford a place like that boarding house. And if she had been half as good at whoring as she was at baking, he could believe it.

He pinched off a piece of the cake, put it in his mouth, and savored it. He made himself wait three minutes before he pinched off the next piece. If he could, Hiram Mitchell decided, he would make the cake last through the hanging. If there was one thing in the world he could call his own it was self-control. Matthew had never had any, really. The both of them would have been dead at the end of a rope years ago if Hiram Mitchell hadn't had self-control.

Matthew had stuck with the rules, though, even when he had started drinking too much. No matter what they had done, they had never gone back to the place they had done it. They had seen a lot of the country that way, and since there was a lot of country to see, they had never been bored. And they couldn't take anything that someone might recognize later and raise suspicions. That had meant they only ever, really, took money and food, but those two things and the freedom to go where he pleased was all any reasonable man could want for himself.

Hiram Mitchell put the next piece of cake in his mouth and told himself he was going to hold it there for thirty seconds before he swallowed. While he waited, he grabbed his canteen and pulled the cork. The cake didn't need any water to go down nicely, but waiting on the hanging was making him thirsty. When the time was up, water and cake found a welcome home in his belly. That old woman surely could bake, he thought.

Hiram Mitchell wasn't angry with Matthew. Not even that morning when he had woken to find that his partner had packed up and left in the night. Matthew had taken to drinking too much and wondering aloud whether they wouldn't be better off finding steady work on a ranch somewhere. Hiram Mitchell had told him they'd talk about it when Matthew was sober, but they never did. And, at some point, it seemed like Matthew was never sober, really. Still, so long as Matthew never broke the rules, Hiram Mitchell had been content to have him along.

Without Matthew along, it had been harder to do some things and impossible to do others. But because he had self-control, Hiram Mitchell had gotten along just fine. He had worked when he needed to and refused to when he was flush. Eventually, his travels had brought him to this area. About three miles west of town there was a farm that had caught Hiram Mitchell's eye. It had been that time when the harvest had been taken in and the farmers were taking their bounty to sell. A good time, because there were fewer men in the homes. At the farm that had caught Hiram Mitchell's eye, there had been one woman who had looked to be all by herself. In a copse of trees where he wasn't likely to be seen, Hiram Mitchell had dismounted and had set himself to watching the farm to make sure. By the time night had come, he hadn't seen any sign of man or dog on the property and he had been satisfied.

When the lights in the house had been put out, Hiram Mitchell had sneaked to a window and had peeked in. When he hadn't seen anyone unexpected, just the woman in her bed, he had gone to the front door. The door had been unlocked, and as he had gone in he had said a silent thanks for trusting country folk.

Hiram Mitchell had left that house two hours later with a sack of bread, roast chicken, and potatoes. The few coins he had found were in his pocket. As he had mounted his horse he had been satisfied that the rules were working. He had gone east with no plans to return. It wasn't until he had been in Durango for about a week that he had heard any news, and, damn him, if it wasn't a small world. The papers were saying that Matthew Swanson had been arrested for the murder of his wife. Matthew Swanson who had a farm that, out of all the farms, Hiram Mitchell had sneaked into because there hadn't been a man around to interfere.

Hiram Mitchell had stayed on in Durango doing odd jobs and living in that boarding house in order to keep an eye on the proceedings. He hadn't been sure, at first, that this was the Matthew he knew, but the newspapers had printed descriptions of the accused and then he had been convinced. The papers had put the story on the front page for weeks, repeating details about how Matthew had shown up at the jail, his shirt soaked in blood, and quite drunk. After the sheriff had had a look around the farm, he had come to the conclusion that Matthew had

killed his wife in a drunken rage. The papers had liked to make
a deal out of Matthew being new to the area and how other
folks hadn't known much about him. They had explained away
his coming into town to report the crime as the faulty reasoning
of a drunken man.

Matthew Swanson didn't need to be drunk to have faulty reasoning, Hiram Mitchell knew. He figured he had a pretty good
idea of what had happened. How Matthew had come home with
his proceeds to show his wife. How he had thrown himself, in
tears, on his wife's corpse. How he probably had had a bottle
hidden away where Hiram Mitchell hadn't been able to find it,
like old drunks do, and had tried to drown his grief. And how
he had probably figured that, because his conscience was clean
in this regard, he had nothing to worry about from the law.

It hadn't been long before there was a trial and the jury had
taken little time to find Matthew guilty. The prosecutor had told
a lurid story about a depraved man whose real nature, despite
outward appearance, had inevitably resulted in the death of a
beloved local woman. Who could really know such a person?
Well, Hiram Mitchell knew. And he knew even more than
before that juries were not to be trusted. But they had done him
a favor, really. Because they had Matthew, they weren't looking
for anyone else. And because they were going to hang him and
wash their hands of it all, Hiram Mitchell could break his rule
and return to the place where he had done a thing, since no one
could be suspicious now.

Hiram Mitchell saw a group of men come out of the jail. He
was too far away to see Matthew's face properly, but his head
was held high. Hiram Mitchell approved. The sheriff led the way
to the scaffold. Deputies flanked Matthew and a minister stood
behind him. Before the men could climb onto the scaffold, a
mangy dog jumped up there and hopped around like he wanted
to play. Some in the crowd laughed and pointed as the sheriff
and one of the deputies chased the dog off the platform.

The deputies placed Matthew on the trapdoor. One of them
stayed by him while the other walked over to the lever for the
door. The sheriff held up a paper and began to talk. Hiram
Mitchell was too far away to hear him properly, but figured
the charges and punishment were being read out. And when
that was done, he figured they'd offer Matthew a chance for

some last words, which they did. While he was talking, Hiram Mitchell thought back to the things they had done together. He wondered if that minister had been any comfort to Matthew, who had sometimes talked like he believed that God was good, even after he had done a bad thing.

Hiram Mitchell didn't know, himself. He had never been able to decide one way or the other. But then he had a thought. He pictured a daisy in his head and he plucked a petal from it. He decided this would do just fine. Hiram Mitchell plucked the next petal. "God is good." He plucked again. "No, He ain't." He kept plucking and, since this daisy was in his head, he knew he had as many petals as were needed. He kept as steady a pace as he knew how. He didn't want to cheat. There was an important question to be answered. Whichever petal was the last to be plucked wasn't up to him, after all, he just needed to pluck it.

Matthew stopped talking and the deputy put the noose around his neck. Hiram Mitchell felt himself flush, but he forced himself to keep pace. A nervous smile came on his face. When the deputy pulled the lever, Hiram Mitchell twitched like it had been his neck in that noose, but he soon had himself under control. He could see that the rope hadn't broken Matthew's neck and the condemned man was jerking and kicking like a drowning man trying impossibly to find the surface. Hiram Mitchell plucked.

"God is good."

"No, He ain't"

And when Matthew's boots had kicked their last and he was still except for the swing of the rope, Hiram Mitchell had his answer. He slapped the neck of his horse. "God is good". And, of course, He was. He looked out for those He loved. That was why there were things in the world like vanilla cake, unlocked doors, and hangman's nooses. And wasn't Hiram Mitchell loved and looked out for? Wasn't he a blessed part of His creation?

Hiram Mitchell turned his horse, there being nothing more to see now that Matthew was dead. He wanted to find a quiet place where he could laugh as long and loud as he cared to without anyone wanting to know why. He put the last of the vanilla cake in his mouth and put his spurs to the horse. With a heart lighter than he had ever known, Hiram Mitchell rode out into God's good creation.

Small Things

by Desmond Everest Fuller

I could do small things. Last spring, I shelled the whole pea patch. Mom kissed my green-stained palms and told me I was good. I could sing under my breath so the prairie wind would not hear. Every day I sang as I carried water to the house, the naked blue sky like a sea held aloft by God.

"Water in the bucket, water in the bucket from the well. Walk on tiptoe, walk on by, just walk so the water don't spill."

Sometimes the moon swam in the bucket as I carried it across the yard past the sheep pen full of them, dumb and square-eyed in their dirty wool that turned my guts with the scent of lanolin. The Nebraska night was so vast, I feared some force would pull me over the edge of it if I lingered too long in it. So I sloshed my hurried way to the porch and the seam of light under the door.

A single oil lamp burned upon our table, throwing wan light to the corners. Dad, Mom, Sister and I would gather here to sup. Our dog, Sampson would lick up potato peels fallen beneath the table skirt and be sick, whimpering from his rug through the night.

While Sampson rested his head atop my feet beneath the table, Dad read from the Bible and stroked Sister's hand. The three of us sat and listened to Dad's drone, dry as salt-wood. He read of the story of Peter's three denials of Jesus, and the Lord's foretelling of Peter's lies. Dad held a finger aloft, pointed up into the gloom of the rafters. He closed the Bible and stared into the grain of the table.

"Mendacity." He uttered.

In my bed that night I tried to lie. I tried to say I was seven when I was still two months left in six. I tried to say I was an empty vessel and could be filled to the brim with the water of the Lord.

"Water in the bucket, water in the bucket."

I wondered at how my utterances could attract God's notice.

Sister peered at me from beneath her sheets--hair spread upon the pillow like corn-silk. She told me not to worry, that she did not believe God heard the prayers of little creatures like children, or the field mouse under the shadow of the owl's wing. That she prayed for Dad's soul to be pure and good like water through limestone. That he would find God in the grass. But she did not believe God heard.

This sounded of blasphemy, but she was Sister, and she was fourteen, and I trusted no one more.

Dad settled in Nebraska because he said it was free of corruption. He had worked a timber camp out west in Orr-e-gone, and Warshing-ton where he said the moss grew like a plague and metal rusted overnight. The wind in Nebraska was clean, the grass swayed in time with the turning of the earth and the air was dry and flat as the ground over which it flew.

Maybe if I hadn't tried to lie, it would not have happened.

I was trusted to take Sampson on morning walks down the dirt lane on my own. Every day I tried to walk farther to see how brave I could be, and would hug his neck when the wind picked up with a hateful wail that put him to whimpering. I had walked several miles, my mind a tangle with the question of God's ear and judgment. Why did sister pray for Dad's soul?

I was looking back at our footprints in the dust when the riders came upon me. The men atop the horses cast long shadows like wavering strings of molasses off tin spoons. They sat and stared while I stood quiet, and Sampson panted next to me in the dust. They chewed tobacco, their grasshopper mouths jawing in the dust. I lowered my gaze away from the beards and sun-browned leather cheeks. Only the wind spoke.

The foremost rider clicked his steed forward several paces, iron horseshoes sounding in the dense quiet like poplar branches snapping in a freeze.

"Son, that's one poor excuse for a mutt. Like he's walkin' meat."

Soft laughter like the scratch of sandpaper.

"Anyplace up the way for a man to rest? Bite of grub? A

friendly hearth?"

And with all of heaven watching I shook my head three times like Peter. Mendacity.

The man leaned low on the pommel of his saddle, squinting as if the light hurt. "We ain't seen nothin' out here. It's days ridin' back to anything."

He pulled himself upright to survey the surrounding pastel hills. "This the kind of country a man could lose direction. Lose hisself, forget what's a man for. And here you are. A boy walkin' his sorry-ass dog. Like a goddamn minor miracle."

The rider grinned dirty yellow gold and blinked once, slow as snow falling.

"Boy, I ain't all sure you ain't a mirage. This company's been known to see things, to fall prey to demonic visitations. So you go on and tell me what's up the way. Assure me my lucidity."

Steel winked in the sun bent off their bandoleers. I hoped to feel the presence of some angels, but instead I felt the emptiness of the Nebraska plains and that the edge of everything had pulled itself upon me. And I was mute in that vacuous space, staring down at the shadows of those men.

"Well, no matter," he said. "I guess I don't trade much in mens' notions of lucidity no how. Take care of that dog now, you hear?"

Horse hooves clopped, pulled the viscus shadows by the root. My eyes screwed shut, I heard the shuffle of leather and spurs. I smelled the sharp stink of horse sweat. Sampson whined low in the dust at my feet.

In the empty lane, in the waving grass, I wondered if the riders had been there at all. There was nothing here that breathed. Only the grass. God was not in this place. Not with me.

The riders' crescent tracks made a school in the dust, fleck in streaks of tobacco juice. I followed them up the lane until I heard the air crack, like a thunder warning, like Dad's rifle, the air split with gunfire.

I cut from the lane, running into the grass. I heard my own

voice chanting in the clapping of breath hot and strained in my lungs. "Water in the bucket, water, water in the bucket."

There were shouts of men. Yips of twisted fancy. I came upon our home and the backs of horses standing in a row between the house and the sheep pen. A wedge-shaped rock jutted from the ground and caught my foot so I tumbled and lay low in the grass. I held Sampson against my chest, holding to his weight, worried my fear would carry me like a feather into the sky and I'd never hold anything again.

Black smoke emanated from the clapboard windows, carrying screams and shouts onto the air. Two more shots. Then, from the back of the house flew a streak of light. And I watched Sister, her back and shoulders harried in flames, run from the cabin. Sprigs of grass caught fire briefly in her wake, a burning trail from the back door to where she fell as the last shot crackled, her arms spread wide as if she were falling into a welcome embrace.

The riders moved on, taking what few things one might consider valuable. The cabin smoked and stank. Burnt hair and blood and cloth. I lay rooted in the grass, watching smoke curl and fade against the void of blue. Two days I didn't move, sleeping in my imprint, feeling the pull of the moon walking above me, and the ants marching across my wrist on their way to somewhere less lonely.

I could not dig a grave deep enough for Sister, who lay in the flowering clover behind the cabin in her scorched dress. I could hold Sampson's neck and cry into the thick fur behind his ears. I could fetch a bucket from the post at the corner of the sheep pen and pull water for him to drink. I could wash Sister's cold face with droplets from my fingers. I could close her eyes that were staring like glass up at the stars that were vast and dying like sparks in God's palm. I could see their light glowing silver on the grass around me and wonder if this was God coming to tell me why I was not in his kingdom. I could watch the sun shining down the lane to swim up the side of the burned cabin. I could breathe. I could do small things.

Dead or Alive

by Mickey Collins

"So what do you do for a living?"

"You could say I'm in law enforcement."

"Like a deputy? A sheriff? Do you carry a gun? Can I see your badge?"

"Hold up, little darling. It's nothing like that. You know the wanted posters?"

"Like the ones they have at the post office? Or around town if he's truly a bad guy?"

"Just like that. You see, I'm the guy that draws their faces." Maybe I should stop leading with the "law enforcement" line. I could see the disappointment down her face. "Should we pay now? I could get you take you home now…"

"No, it's fine. I'm having a good time. I want to hear more about you."

And that's how I met Trixie, the love of my life.

After I started going steady with Trixie we started catching a lot more criminals and they said it was 'cause my wanted posters had more lifelike quality to them. Even though once or twice I must admit that I added a smile to a criminal accidentally, but I couldn't help myself. I was just so darned happy. That is until the day *he* walked in.

I was at my desk when the sheriff came in with him.

"Hey, Mr. Sketch Artist. We've taken this guy's story. Would you mind sitting down with him to get his sketch? I want to get this guy's face up lickitisplit. He's a real bad egg."

"Of course, Sheriff Showalter."

While the sheriff showed the witness to the chair, I got a new broadsheet and set up my space. "What did this guy do?" I asked.

He looked hard at me.

"It helps me to pick out the pencils I use, depending on the crime he committed," I said.

"Murder," he said, without taking his eyes off me. He was angry, and rightfully so it seemed.

"The big one." As I sharpened my chosen pencil to a fine point he asked how we would get started.

"I like to start with the eyes, I suppose, but if there are any outstanding features you remember--scars, that sort of thing--that's a good place to start, too."

He stared, lost in thought.

"Take your time," I offered, while I sketched out a basic oval shape for a head, the ears, and the usual stuff heads had. Witnesses often needed a moment to recollect.

"He had small eyes," he said at last. "Average mouth, high cheekbones, dark hair, no beard…"

We continued on like this for about half an hour. I was totally engrossed in the work. Never had I had a witness who could remember so much detail about the criminal. If only this man could be a witness to more crimes.

After we had finished, I put the portrait aside and asked if he needed any water or anything. He declined and instead asked, "Are you going to put the 'Dead or Alive' thing on there?"

I shrugged. "That's up to Sheriff Showalter. I just draw the pictures. I'll ink this one and then hand it off to get it printed up. In my experience most murderers are only 'Dead'."

"You know, I never understood the 'Dead or Alive' thing until just recently. I had a girl I was seeing back home. She moved out west before me. The plan was for her to wait until I got out here and then we'd buy a little farm and start raising a family. Well it took me a little longer to finish up my business than I expected and when I got out here, I found she's with someone else now.

And I just don't know if I want her dead or alive."

"What about this murderer?"

"I reckon that all murderers deserve death," he said. "Especially ones who break hearts."

"But if he's taken alive, then you get have him brought to justice. He can sit in a jail cell to think on what he's done wrong."

"Hmm," he said. And then he got his coat and walked out.

I grabbed the sketch and decided I'd finish it up at home after getting some of Trixie's food in my belly.

Later that night I was working by oil lamp at my desk. Usually inking was the easiest part, but something was stopping me from working as I normally did. Trixie's hand on my shoulder made me jump in my seat.

"Didn't mean to frighten you," she said. "I just wanted to see if you were ready for bed." She looked over the sketch. "That looks really good. Are you going to draw me next?"

"What do you mean?"

"Well, it's a self portrait ain't it? If you draw one of me we can hang them up in the parlor on either side of daddy's Winchester."

I took a look at the face before me. That's where my hesitation was coming from. Staring back at me was me. I spent so many days looking at other people's faces that I didn't even realize the resemblance this one had to me. I gave Trixie a peck on the cheek and told her I'd be to bed in a moment. Once she was out of the room again, I set to finishing up the drawing.

The next day I handed in the completed portrait to the sheriff. He gave it a once-over. "You don't happen to have a brother, do you?"

"No, sir. Why do you ask?"

"Well this fella here looks just like you, except for that he's got a big ol' mustache." He laughed.

I laughed as well. "You know, I didn't even realize."

I spent the rest of the day holed up in my room, organizing my inks and thinking about the portrait. Was there really someone out there committing crimes who looked just like me? I had to give him a mustache, I reasoned. Or else the sheriff would come to me and start asking me questions. I did not do well under pressure. I'd seen many men crack under the sheriff's tough questioning.

No less than twenty four hours after my initial sit down with the witness and the sheriff comes and sits down with me again. "Now, I don't want to be questioning your professional code or anything," he said. "But did you add a mustache to the portrait you drew of that murderer?"

"Of course I did. Remember, you even said how he could be my mustachioed brother."

"That's not what I mean. I mean that the witness is saying that he never told you the murderer had a mustache and now on the wanted poster he has a mustache."

I stayed silent.

"I'm going to need you to redo the sketch, this time without a mustache. And I need it by the end of the day."

"Yes, sir."

The sheriff left the wanted poster that had been posted on my desk. I used that as a reference to draw up a new, clean-shaven portrait. There was something uncanny about seeing your face, drawn in your own hand, paired with the words "Wanted Dead."

I paused outside the sheriff's door. Although I had seen innocent men walk away before, more often than not the men I drew on these posters were sent to the gallows or else taken out by gunslingers and bountymen. But surely a guilty man wouldn't have a hand in his own sentencing.

I handed off the new portrait to the sheriff. He gave the drawing a once-over and then looked back at me. "Maybe don't leave town, ya hear?"

I gave a laugh, as only an innocent man could.

As I left the sheriff's office I bumped into Deputy Black. "Hi there," I said. "Do you happen to know where that witness from yesterday is staying?" I drew a quick sketch of him on a piece of paper.

"Well I reckon that he's got a room at the Pony's Rest, like most every other drifter who comes through town."

I'd never been to the Pony's Rest before, it wasn't really what I was in to, but the madam at the front greeted me like an old friend. I supposed it was her job, afterall, to make every guest feel welcome like that.

"Do you recognize this man?" I asked, holding up my sketch. "I need to ask him a few questions."

"Maybe I do," she said after a drag on her cigarette. "Maybe he's here, maybe he's not."

I'd been with the sheriff's office long enough to have heard about their experiences with non-cooperative types. From my billfold I pulled out a $10 bill and slid it over to her.

"He must be very important," she said. Another cigarette drag as she stuff the bill into her corset. "But he's not here. One of the girls overheard him yelling about some poster or something and he stormed out an hour ago. She tried to cheer him up, you know, but he pushed her away saying that she wasn't Trixie. But we don't have any Trixies here."

Trixie?

I ran off toward home. When I arrived, the front door was wide open. "Trixie?" I yelled from the doorway, but there was no response. The Winchester was removed from the wall. One of the floorboards creaked from the bedroom. My heart raced. With nothing to defend myself, I moved forward. "Trixie?" I called again.

I couldn't hear any noises coming from the bedroom. I pushed it open.

Trixie was on the bed. Blood flowed from her chest onto the sheets. "Trixie…"

The witness rocked back in forth in the chair across from her, holding the rifle like a baby.

"I've decided," he said. "Dead is better."

And then the sound of a gunshot.

Little Cowboys

by Carson Everson

A defunct suburban holdout, condemned to demolition, which had thrived as our greatest embodiment of the American Dream, was continually terrorized by a roguish group of little cowboys.

Crimes of the little cowboys include, and are not limited to the following:

snot-nosing;

cruel indecency;

public drunkenness;

father-murder.

Approaches to exterminating the little cowboys include, and are not limited to the following:

trick-murals;

shooting them from a great distance;

poisoning the water supply.

We used metal walls to blot out the sun. We raised them high. Hell, it took the little bastards out of the picture two blessed weeks. Any time a cowboy awoke (and no cowboy wakes up at a regular time), he rubbed his eyes, saw it was still dark, and closed his eyes again.

It was the girls who unfortunately saved them. It started with one. It took just one suburban girl to fall in love with a cowboy. And this then roused the other girls. This, their first exposure to love, which consequently disappeared all our girls to the realm of the cowboys.

Some have suggested the cowboys have burrowed small holes, not unlike legions of termites. I have used a telescope. And I have seen into the sides of these hills. I see no evidence of cave dwellings. It's the sewers. I think they're living right under us, smelling us, sniffing us, watching our every move.

We in fear everyday we are living. The inevitable Rule of the Cowboy.

I have dreams of their lassos, circling and circling in the sky, then coming down and squeezing around my neck. Then they drag me, kicking and gagging, into the hills and away from my beautiful front home with a garage, a putting green and a koi pond.

I imagine them to look like weevils in cowboy hats as the dig up from the sewers and claim us from the bottom up. They will kill the men. We, naturally, are the little cowboys' biggest threat. They will kill their own fathers and the fathers of the girls they have stolen.

And my wife, what if she, unaware, continues to dote upon the little cowboy? Who am I to her then, if I survive? If I am wrong and they don't beat by brains in with a stone? I will be nothing but a stranger. And I will poke about at the outer walls of what was once my own home.

This is what kept me up at night, not so much the manner of how the cowboys would kill me, but of how much they would come to enjoy my life, when they've come and taken it.

But, consider, why aren't the cowboys reproducing already? At first I thought, well the little cowboys are still, as of yet, incapable of reproduction. They, as boys, disappeared from us ten years ago, that would make them… And this is where it falls apart. And besides, I have watched them (as I've as yet yet waited for my replacement). And they are fully capable of the act, at reckless frequency. No, the boys are surely men, but it's something wrong. It's when we poisoned their water or kept them in night. We made them go dry. The cowboys are incapable of reproduction.

In this respect, we have outfoxed the little cowboys. Even I, at thirty-eight years of youth, am still capable of reproduction. They will not drag their fathers away but keep them in their attics. They will not allow us to come out except at rare times to invigorate the population.

For now, they are finishing up stealing the last of our newborns. We have made attempts at hiding them away, but for the cowboys' all-seeing eye.... I suspect that it's tor survival that they sneak into our bedrooms and replace our children with socks.

I cannot fault them, the tiny cowboys, for their doings are akin to my own, how I won my wife, how I slipped into her home unnoticed and tried on her father's glasses.

Western Denial
by AJD

If I don't have to be awake,
I won't.

Fuck you, and your world.

The west, where the sun sets, is death.
The sun, born in the east, dies in the west.

Fuck you, and your death world. Your endgame.

Dumbfucking rednecks,
and their conservative think tank sugar daddies,
play up the myths. Round and round they go,
manifesting their death destiny again and again.

Fuck your west, your myth of independence, of frontier testing.

You genocidal zombies! Look at the bodies you shot, you in-
fected!
Don't just step over them, on your way to California, to Oregon.
Look into the seeping pus from the wounds you brought on.

Wake, wake into the west.
I won't. If I don't have to be awake, I will not. Fuck you.
And your ten gallon hats.

For I'm the Gravest Sinner

by Robert Eversmann

Two young cowboys are given a rope by their father. The father has decided they have not enough food to feed each other. Only two of them can live, not three. But it's not a father's right to choose.

He left a rope in their room. They had two beds and a wall of cowboys. They liked shooting each other all day.

It does not matter to me much, so long as I've got one to carry on my name. Here you go. The boys spent the afternoon trying to think which one of them deserved to die. They tried to think of the worst thing they'd ever done.

'You killed a cat. I watched you.'

'But I didn't want to. He made me do it.'

'You're right, you're right. That doesn't count.'

'And besides, you killed a dog. That was on purpose.'

He didn't respond.

'Look, I have the knife. It's still in the drawer.'

He pulled out a knife from the drawer with the dog collar. The knife was very small. The accused boy sat laid in bed on his back and stared at the ceiling.

Old West Justice

by Dan Heise

There was a faint buzzing and ringing in Wayne's ears. He shook his head to ignore it, but it persisted in the back of his mind. He adjusted the rope to the other shoulder and continued trudging along. The man at the end of the rope kept struggling and squirming. It was starting to annoy Wayne.

As was the heat. God damn, how was he supposed to get anything done? How did anyone get anything done like this?

Wayne lifted off his hat and wiped his brow. Slowly, he sank to the ground, deciding it was best to rest. He would need to keep his strength up. Wayne got out his canteen and took a long slow drink. As he did, the man at the end of the rope's eyes grew wide. He started squirming even more. Wayne arched an eyebrow and looked at him with amusement.

"Keep on doin' that, and you really won't get any."

The squirming stopped. Wayne chuckled and continued to drink. He stared out at the wide expanse of desert and sighed deeply.

"There's something I love about being out here. Just the… desolate quiet. And it's beautiful out here. It really is." Wayne turned to the man at the end of the rope. "Wouldn't you agree?"

Slowly, dolefully, the man nodded. He didn't take his eyes off the water canteen though.

Wayne got up slowly, and sauntered over to the man. That buzzing, that ringing, was still there. He shook his head to try and dispel it. He stood over the man menacingly, holding the canteen behind his back.

"Now, I couldn't help but notice that you agreed with me, but you didn't happen to even look around at this beautiful landscape that surrounds us. So how could you possibly agree with me?" The man shook his head, fighting against the gag over his mouth.

Wayne continued: "I'm gonna give you one more chance. Go ahead. Look around. Everything is orange and brown and gorgeous in the sun. It'll be setting soon, and you'll get to see a whole other world out here. Ain't it purdy? Isn't this what everyone came out here for? Yet no one enjoys it. Only those who wander out here and take the time to appreciate the places like this. No one around for dozens of miles. It's serene almost. Now, one more time: Isn't it beautiful?"

Wayne stooped over and removed the gag. The man looked around him, seeming to take it all in.

"Yes, sir," he said in a timid voice.

"Now, come on Will, you don't have to call me sir," drawled Wayne. "You can just call me Wayne out here."

Will nodded once. "Yes, Wayne. I understand."

"Good. Glad you understand. You want a little water?" Wayne shook the canteen at him.

"Yes, please."

"You know to respect people. I'll give you that, Will," Wayne said, slowly drawing the top of the canteen. A breeze blew through the sparse vegetation, rattling it unsettlingly. Almost as unsettling as the pause that was now descending between Wayne and Will. Will looked back and forth nervously.

"SOME people. You know how to respect some people," Wayne finished, and poured the water into Will's eyes. Will thrashed about, shaking his head, trying to get the water out of his eyes. Eventually, he started screaming.

"HELP!!! SOMEONE HELP!!!" he hollered at the top of his lungs. Wayne just shook his head.

"Ain't no one around for miles. Now come on. There's a tree coming up here in a handful of miles I'm really itching to show ya."

Wayne put the gag back on Will, hoisted the rope over his shoulder, and continued walking.

About two hours and several miles passed, and Wayne had finally reached his destination: a scraggly tree out in the middle of the desert. He left Will several yards away, and walked over to the tree, his spurs jangling. He looked up at it with awe, almost reverence.

"So many people hung here already. Who knows how many more there will be by the time it's all said and done? Whenever that may be." Wayne touched the rough bark lightly. He heard a crunching noise behind him and turned around. Will was trying to roll away. Wayne shook his head at him.

As he looked at Will rolling around in the dust, the low buzzing came back. The ringing. Wayne put his hands up to temples, pressing hard. It'd been like this for hours now. Ever since he dragged Will out to this god forsaken desert. Finally, it subsided. Wayne glared at Will, who was still trying to roll away. Wayne stalked towards him and put a foot down right on his gut. Will grunted, his eyes watering with pain. Wayne dragged him over to the tree roughly. He threw him against the trunk, and the tree shuttered. Will hit his head hard and cried out through the gag. The tears hadn't stopped. Wayne glared at him. More buzzing and ringing again. He pushed on.

"Will Hart. You have been found guilty of the rape of my daughter, and therefore I sentence you to hang by the neck until dead. Do you have anything to say for yourself before the sentence is carried out?" Wayne ripped the gag off of Will. Will looked around in bewilderment.

"What? Rape? Please, Wayne, I have no idea what you're talking about, we were boyfriend and girlfriend for god's sake!-" Will pleaded with Wayne, but he cut him short.

"You have besmirched her honor, Will!"

"Premarital sex is not besmirching her honor, you old antiquated bastard! What the fuck is wrong with you??" Will yelled at him, now enraged. The pain was going away, and he was emboldened by it. That, and the fact that Wayne was clearly insane. "You drag me out here for hours, I'm fucking dirty and bloody and bruised up, and your plan is to hang me? What year do you live in? Are you seriously gonna hang every single one of her boyfriends that she has for the rest of her life?"

"She's 16! She's not able to make these decisions by herself! You obviously had to take her forcefully!" Wayne was getting hot now, his blood boiling. His hand reached instinctively for the gun that was holstered there.

"She is fully capable of making her own decisions! What, you think just because I'm 19 that means she's not old enough for me? Fuck you, old man! If she can drive, she's allowed to make her own decisions about who she fucks! And she chose me! So fuck you!"

The buzzing swelled in Wayne's ears. The ringing also. He couldn't take it anymore. He took the gun out, and fired it into Will's leg. The shot echoed across the desert. Will screamed out.

"AAAHHH!!! FUCK!!!!!!!" Will was openly crying now. He tried to take deep breaths but found it difficult. The pain was excruciating. He looked up at Wayne. His breathing was labored. Everything was agony. "Please, Wayne, don't do this. I'm sorry. I won't see her ever again. I'll leave forever."

"It's too late for that," Wayne said, turning away. The gunshot had temporarily gotten rid of the buzzing, but it was still there in the background of everything. Will looked up at Wayne.

"Answer your fucking phone already, your psychopath, it's been ringing for hours."

Wayne went over to Will and hit him over the head with the butt of his gun. Will slumped over on the ground. Wayne walked away a few paces, and took his cell phone out of his pocket.

"This is Wayne."

"Dad? It's Grace. Where are you? You left me home alone."

"Your mother isn't home?"

"No, she had to leave for a teacher meeting! Remember?" Grace's voice was annoyed.

"Oh, I'm sorry sweet pea. I had entirely forgotten. I didn't mean to leave you alone. Were you able to get dinner?" Wayne was genuinely sorry. He didn't mean to abandon his daughter like this.

"No, that's why I've been calling. That and you just kinda left out of nowhere. You weren't answering and I had to take some money out of the jar for gas and some fast food. I hope that was ok."

"Of course it is. I'm sorry again, Grace. I just got a sudden call for work and had to leave. I'll be back later tonight, ok? I promise."

"All right. Should I let mom know? She's been trying to get ahold of you too."

"If you would. Thanks, Grace. Love you." Wayne meant it.

"Love you too, Dad. I'll see you tonight. Hope work goes ok."

Grace hung up, and Wayne looked at his phone dolefully. He didn't want to have to leave her alone. He didn't ever want her to suffer. But she was growing up. Capable of driving, capable of going out and getting fast food on her own. Maybe it was time to let her test her newfound wings, the wings that came with being an adult. Wayne stared at the unconscious form of Will for a long time.

Finally, Wayne sighed. That time would come at some point. But it wasn't yet.

He slung a rope over a branch of the tree.

The Nightmare
by Robert Eversmann

The cowboy built a small playground for the orphans. The orphans swarmed him. He picked them up on his shoulders. He made them fly like airplanes.

The cowboy's bones grew brittle. The children pointed their hands like guns at him when they saw him.

The cowboy had a nightmare. The children were using him to build the playground. One orphan with a leg, one orphan with an arm. They were hammering the nails. Another orphan opened the cowboy's mouth. *Yeehaaaawwww*, he said.

West

by Ariel Kusby

A rough place I return to often. The wildness of blood between my legs. A savage quiet when the frogs finally sleep. Heartbreak like hard candy. Slow orange days slicked down with aloe. My feet fighting with the sand. Hammering stakes down. Always conquering something or other. Ribbons of fool's gold under my boots. Eyes open underwater. Fires burning ancient forests down to the dirt. The claustrophobia of open landscape. My own animal tracks. Deep pockets of rock. Geothermal pools of hot green bloom. Static on my skin and in my hair. The rope trick of thirst. A reminder of something I've forgotten. Woman with a gun. The blood orange that is darker than you'd expect inside. A body in the distance. A secret with a heartbeat.

The Sore

by Ben Crowley

My brother's ankle grew like a balloon. He dragged it around and bumped into things.

'What's happening to me?' he said.

He said it always and threw his hands down, having kicked over a train set.

'I blame you,' he said. 'You're a bad brother.'

Once I blindfolded him and he caught his ankle on a carpet nail. It leaked but it wouldn't get any smaller. I pressed on it for him. This put him to sleep.

In the town center, they made my brother coffins almost everyday. He was infamous, my brother. I'd pass by the coffin maker, whose eyes were like stones.

'Tap. Tap. Tap,' he'd say. 'I'll make your brother a fine coffin.' He was creaky, even for as old as he was. 'I'm ready for him, any day now. Tap. Tap. Tap.'

My brother was not well liked because of his role in the city as a policy maker.

The mail piled up at our door. There were so many rules in place, I couldn't explain enough to them. They were sending so many questions. I could not replace my brother. My work is not my brother's and I dreamt I was being eaten by snow.

My brother stayed up all night playing the saw. This, I didn't mind. He was swollen and this kept him up at night. He was spectral, my brother. He wandered the house like an orphan.

This kept me awake. What had I done? Deprived of sleep, I lost my ability of distinction. Reality became fantasy and this affected my letters of policy, consequently too, public life and my brother's reputation.

The townspeople stopped leaving their homes, preferring deep privacy.

One night I came downstairs to see my brother guzzling bowls full of beer. He was in the cellar. I heard him clinking around down there, in a nightmare, he drank until his tumor outgrew him. He begged like a prisoner. I held his head up right to feed him the beer.

When his face was at its palest and his mouth dripped like a snake's, he whispered things unholy in my ear.

'Mother's inside,' he'd say.

'What?' I'd say.

'Listen,' he'd say. 'It's unbelievable.'

'You left me in here to rot,' she said.

'Mother?' I said.

Something shifted inside the ankle. 'I'm not a mother to you, but a festering wound.'

In a nightmare, my brother tended to my fever. Then he strangled me. He cited the tumor as his motivation.

In another nightmare, the whole town came to see my brother. They abandoned their cars. They came in, pulling pieces from the ankle. They asked him how he was doing and was recovering, then returned home with handfuls of my brother.

In his own version of this nightmare, my brother, always the diplomat, attempted placating mothers while they screamed at him and beat him because he was holding and devouring their children.

I passed by the coffin maker on the way to the mail. He said, 'I've made many coffins now for your brother. I've made so many, I've begun resizing the dead bodies that come in. I make them like your brother. So they can fit inside his coffin. I can make no other kind of coffin. I only make coffins for your brother. I've made hundreds. Would you like to see?'

He took me into his house.

'I can't get your brother off my mind. I see him and my hands move on their own. I'll take you in here. You should see.'

He took me into his work room, which was full of coffins for my brother, then into his basement, which was also full of coffins for my brother. 'They are so hard to make. You brother is strange man.'

'You know his name?'

'Yes, it's your name too. Your name, like his, is in my mouth. I can't get his name out of my mouth. I do not drink the milk. *He* drinks the milk. I do not take the shit but he takes the shit. I'm afraid that if your brother dies, I will cease to exist. Help me. Please. Please,' he said. He came close to me.

'I cannot help you,' I said.

He came yet closer to me. He swiped at me. This man was very small, the coffin-maker. He said my name, my brother's name. He repeated it. He could say nothing else. He reached at me as if there was nothing else to hold onto.

'I will not help you,' I said. 'I refuse.'

And so I did, and so rightfully so. I would not help this man, as this man was a lunatic of policy, and nothing could be done.

Memories from Oklahoma

by Timothy Arliss O'Brien

The wild Wild West isn't so wild anymore.

It's now mostly parking lots, suburbs, and shopping malls.

But I did fuck a cowboy once.

His horse wasn't as big as he said,
and I would have mistaken it for a petting zoo donkey in a
parade.

Idk how he could take it to the rodeo.

And he was terrible with a lasso.

At least on me.

But who would be able to lasso me?

I'm the 21st century Wild West:
Weed, psychedelics, and new age philosophies,
Conquering the vast plains of the sub-conscience.

Maybe I just fucked a cowboy to brag about it.

The Executioner

by Robert Eversmann

The cowboy is fired by the executioner.

The cowboy drags out a body as proof. It was grey and hard as a rock.

'This is no dead body, this is an Egyptian,' says the executioner.

The cowboy feigns a heart attack and asks the executioner to hang him.

'End it for me, for I don't have the courage,' he said.

The executioner is deceived, tied up by the cowboy.

The cowboy posts the following on every saloon: "THE EX-ECUTIONER WILL BE EXECUTED."

The cowboy dresses like a king.

'So you're the king?' says a man to the cowboy. The man is eating a lollipop.

'I didn't know a cowboy could be king?'

'Anybody could be the king, sire,' said the king. 'Even you.'

The king gave his crown up to the man. The man became the king.

Under this new king, many executioners were employed. They were worked all through the day and all through the night and still the blood was only paralleled by the executioners' sweat.

The cowboy returned.

'What have you done with your power?' he asked.

'I've reorganized the state,' said the king.

The cowboy drew his gun.

The king drew his gun. The king of the cowboys.

'Long live the king,' declared the executioner, unleashing the guillotine on the final evildoer.

The executioner is totally alone.

Old El Dorado in the Devil's Pass

by Nicholas Yandell

The expression on his face never changes, as the sun goes down. I holler at him a few times, kick him at least once, but it doesn't matter; he just absorbs it with the bare minimum motions to still register as living…

Since there's no traversing the Devil's Pass in the darkness, camping here for the night's inevitable. I won't sleep though; no matter how much I need it; not with him this close by; even if he's all tied up. As I'm growing weary though, and the hours go on, I really don't know why I'm still letting him live.

I 'spose that killin' him would require me to drag him away from camp so as not to spook my horse; I don't have that kind of energy right now. There's something else beyond that though; something unfinished between the two of us.

I don't really know what I expected our final skirmish to be like, but I didn't picture the formidable Levi Dumont, best gunfighter 'round these parts, being all broken and helpless, with no horse, no guns, nothing. Why should the last of the McRaes meet the last of the Dumonts under such anticlimactic circumstances? Surely no one will bother tellin' stories or writing ballads about this final showdown.

Anyway, it's growing so dark that I can't even see the expression on his face anymore. I light a small fire, castin' light on his body, but his head's still just hanging down, so I get up and kick him off the rock. He's unable to catch himself, falling face first into the dirt, where he doesn't move. I holler at him sayin':

"Don't even think about sleeping! As soon as the sun rises, your life is over! Whether that happens real fast or painfully slow is my decision, but I'll let you say what you need to rest your soul; you better speak up now though."

He raises his head and his voice emerges slowly, cracked and not quite audible. "Louder!" I shout, and he manages to muster the word: "water". I sneer at him. "The little water I have, wasted on a Dumont? That's a rich one."

Dropping his head, he says nothing more. So I sigh, take one of my last canteens with just a swig or two left in it, shove it in his face, and he drinks it with obvious relief. After the last drops are gone, I rip it away sayin': "Well, anything else?"

He pauses for a long time and I'm thinkin' maybe he's fallen asleep again, but eventually, out of his mouth comes the words:

"Everything could have been different you know?"

"What the hell does that mean?"

"I'm just saying, if we didn't have Dumont and McRae attached to our names, we'd have been just Levi and Silas; two lonely kids playing *Old El Dorado* under that big pine tree. Lying here, waitin' on death, I've been thinkin' an awful lot about that.

Well, I'm just thinkin' that this day of scorchin' sun has given Levi that heat-stroke delirium, until suddenly it hits me what the hell he's talking about. Then he opens his eyes, and in the moonlight I get this flash of a boy I once knew; that same brown cowlick castin' that deep shadow 'cross his left eye and the lines of his crooked smile still visible in the firelight. Someone I swear I'd forgotten even existed, whom I met by accident when we were both just schoolhouse age…

I'd been waitin' around with my pa, who was trading goods in town. He'd sent me on another errand to get supplies, but I knew he wasn't leavin' soon so I was in no rush to head back. I saw Levi sittin' there, sprawled out on the ground, waitin' by some horses in the shade of that big pine. As I passed by, he hollered at me:

"Howdy, friend! I'm Levi Dumont! What's your name?"

"Uh… Howdy. I'm Silas McRae."

"Nice to make your acquaintance! You look as bored as I am. You wanna play a game?"

I shrugged. "Sure; I guess."

"It's called *Old El Dorado* and it's my favorite!"

He explained the rules as he placed a bunch of sticks into

rectangles, picked up some rocks to toss, and also some pine needles to keep the count. It was confusing at first, but I caught on real quick and we played for what must have been hours, chattin' all the while.

I asked him: "You from this town?"

"Nah. Just arrived in these parts. You?"

"We're in for the day, from just north of here."

"We might be headed that way in the near future. You come into town often?"

"Every week, with my pa, selling livestock at the market."

"Yeah? We're a ranchin' family too. Had to leave our place a day's east of here. Draught finally got us. Now we're looking to settle up your way."

"I'm glad. I hope I'll see you often! I don't really know anyone else my age."

"Well, we should be here most Saturdays. You wanna meet here next week? Middle of the day? I oughta be able to get away by then?"

"Yeah! That'd be mighty fine!"

After that, we kept chatting, until finally I had to say: "Levi, I gotta head out".

"Okay Silas. It was real nice to meet you, I'll see you next week my friend."

"Yeah. I'll see ya real soon!" I reached out my hand, but he surprised me and embraced with a hug, which made me smile real wide.

We continued to meet week after week whenever our families came to market. After heading off on our errands, we'd keep a look out for each other and when I'd see that cowlicked face and crooked smile, I'd feel myself instantaneously brighten up. We'd start with some games of *Old El Dorado*, talk about our lives, and share our lunches with each other, staying as long as we could, even risking getting whupped by our pas, who were waitin' on us. We always managed to make excuses though; never even tellin' our parents about each other, and these times with Levi became what I looked forward to most every week, especially as the tensions grew around the McRae ranch.

Some months after Levi and I first met, I kept hearing the Dumont name being thrown out in fits of rage from various family members. I was real curious to talk to Levi about all this when I finally made it to the pine. He was there with a horse and as soon as he saw me, he hollered saying; "Glad you came Silas! No *El Dorado* for me today. I gotta walk this horse over to the saloon. You can come along with though!"

"You bet!" I said, not really caring what we did. We talked about what was happening with our families, but since we were just kids, no one had really told us much of anything.

When we got to the saloon, the owner took Levi's horse and left to get some goods for his pa. Right after he disappeared, I heard my name yelled from across the way. I was startled and saw my pa lookin' real angry as he made his way over to us.

"Silas! What the hell are you doing? I've been lookin' all over for you!"

"Pa, I was just talkin' to my friend. We were just –"

But Pa cut me off, staring at Levi as he demanded: "Who are you?"

"Uh… I'm Levi Dumont. Nice to make your acquaintance sir."

"You're a Dumont? ... Silas get over here!"

I followed orders, but was pretty confused. He then added: "Go back to the wagon!"

"What?"

Suddenly, my pa pulled out his gun, grabbed Levi and put the gun to his head. Levi was terrified and froze up, with tears streamin' down his face. I ran up to them, grabbed my pa's arm and shouted: "No! Pa, No! He's my friend! He didn't do nothin' to nobody!"

"Shut your mouth Silas! I told you to get on outa here!" Then he shoved me to the ground real hard, and I fell on some rocks bustin' open my lip. When I looked up, pa had Levi face-first on the ground, his foot on top of him and the gun pointed at the back of his head. Pa was yellin': "If I don't kill you now, you'll just grow up into another one of them and that's the last thing this earth needs."

At that time, I heard a click and the saloon owner held a rifle pointed at my pa's head as he was sayin':

"His pa left him here with me and I'm not returning him a dead boy; at least not without his killer's corpse too".

My pa paused, put the gun away, and let Levi loose.

Without another word, he grabbed hold of me, draggin' me off towards our wagon. The last vision I had of young Levi, was the pained and terrified look on his face, staring out at us, as the saloon owner pulled him inside.

When we got back to the wagon, pa took out the bullwhip and tanned my hide harder than he'd ever done in his life. At the end of it, I fell to the ground, bawling my eyes out, and he told me: "I oughta leave you out here for the buzzards to eat. No son of mine will ever defend a Dumont. You are never to see that boy ever again, unless it's to put a bullet in his head; I reckon that's the only way I could ever see you as anything more than the disgrace to our family name."

For weeks after this incident, none of my family would speak to me. I was banned from leaving the ranch for a real long time and they made me do all the worst chores. Even when I did the best I possibly could, I still got taken out to the barn and wh-upped, and all the while, with each lash, my pa would carry on about the Dumonts and what they had done to us, as if bloody-in' up my body, somehow hurt them too.

I guess this whole feud started after the Dumonts moved their ranch to border ours; then some dispute got started over water usage. This led to a Dumont threatening my father, who then threatened Levi of course, and it just escalated from there. It wasn't but a month or so after that day, when we buried my uncle from some sort of skirmish with the Dumonts. Levi's older sister was next to go, taken down in a confrontation just outside of town. We couldn't go much more than a year or so without another McRae or Dumont been buried. I was probably 12 when one of their bullets first grazed my ear, and was 17 when a Dumont died by my hand. Levi though, was a terror to my family, and had already killed two McRae's and landed a half dozen shots on others before he was even 15.

I suppose it's doubtful that this unchecked violence could've ended any other way than it did. No one will likely ever know how the fire started, but the long drought certainly ensured that there wasn't much left of the McRae or the Dumont ranches. I only survived 'cause I was out on an errand, returning just in time to catch glimpse of all the destruction, before the fire forced me out onto this road through the Devil's Pass. From what I saw, I'd gathered I was the only one to make it out alive, but as I was ridin' along this nothin' of rocks and sagebrush, I happened upon Levi, layin' by the side of the road, after being thrown from his horse.

Now here I am, in only the light of the moon, staring at the spots of blood on his cheek, all dried and forgotten. I've had nothin' but enmity for him all these years, but now I can't help but wonder what would have happened if we could've kept on meetin'. I imagine we'd have stayed friends, been best friends even, rather than seeing each other as enemies poisoned against each other by our family names. It made my blood boil; not at him this time, but for what could have been.

I could see us both in some sort of alternate life. Maybe we'd have left that awful town together, like I'd always wanted to; two cowboys crossin' the open frontier, cattle herds in tow. Just riding the days in open prairie air and spending the long nights by the fire. We'd swap stories and laugh, and even throw together an occasional game of *Old El Dorado*, just to remember our younger days.

At that thought, my eyes drift down from the dying flames, and my hands must have been following along or something, 'cause there in the sand were some sagebrush twigs making perfect little rectangles. I look up at Levi; his eyes are all lit up by the fire and he's watchin' me. Despite this whole night, and how I treated him, there's no animosity in his gaze; it's more of just an acceptance of the circumstances with the kind of expression that asks: "Where can we go now?" Without even thinking about it, I take a pebble and chucked it into one of the rectangles and I could swear that when it landed, I caught Levi grinning at me with that same crooked, troublesome smile. Now he's getting up from the dirt and tossing a rock my way, and we're both acting like there are no years between us. We toss a few more stones, until I hear my horse makin' noise behind me and Levi says: "you oughta go check on her". At the sound of another real loud whinny, I turn around, and wake up with a jolt…

Levi's still just lying there, tied up where I left him, so I head over to my horse. A coyote comes tearin' out from the brushes, startlin' me, and by the time I make it over to her, all my full canteens are layin' in the sand, busted open and spilling their water out. I frantically fall to the ground and catch some of the last drops of liquid into my mouth.

Levi stirs awake from all the commotion, but I'm payin' him no heed. Without that water, I won't last out here; I'll be just another victim of these months of drought. I hang my head and then try rein in these thoughts. All I can think of in this moment though is: "what a waste". These pointless years of revenge have led me here, with no water, no hope, just dyin' in the desert with my blood-sworn enemy. I take a deep sigh and strangely realize that it's that last part of this whole thing, which actually makes this situation slightly less bleak.

After another long moment, I look over at Levi, and he's eyein' me closely in this early morning light. I stand up quickly, head over to him and cut his binds. "C'mon. Let's get on our way before the sun hits us hard."

"What do you mean? I don't understand. You're taking me with you?"

"Well, I could kill you, just to satisfy the will of a dead father and a cursed family name; then die alone with the insatiable heat of vengeance burning me hotter than the hottest desert sun, or… we could just bury the hatchet once and for all, because Levi, I never hated you; not really; not when I was allowed to be me. I'd say I liked you better than anyone else I ever met; you're maybe the only real friend I ever had. So if we're gonna die out here, and we probably will, I'd rather live these last hours together in hope that some part of you is that same Levi Dumont I once knew."

He's stunned for a moment, then looks me right in the eyes. "Silas. I tell ya, I've had lots of time lyin' here, thinkin' back on my life, and through it all, those days of playing *Old El Dorado* with you were the memories I kept lingering on the longest. I kept hating myself for being too weak to make my own choices, and joinin' in the feud, and all the blood I spilled, and maybe worst of all, playing the part of an enemy to you; betrayin' someone whom I never saw as anything but a friend. I'm sorry Silas."

"I'm sorry too Levi, but we gotta leave that behind us now. I got no water left, and the sun's not going to be easy on us, so I reckon all we got is a day or so if we're lucky. Still, I say let's leave this place and at least we'll die together on a journey to something better right?"

"Yeah; I guess I'm ready then, my friend."

Offering him my arm, I help him onto my horse, then load her up, get on, and we take off. In our thirst and exhaustion we don't say a whole lot more to each other, but there's a peace in this silence that hasn't been there in ages. As we're ridin' out of the pass though, I feel Levi raising his head and a fleck of his sweat hits my ear.

"You feel that?" He asks.

"Yeah, I guess. Uh. Or, what do ya mean?" Then another drop hits me. More drops after that and quicker now. I stop the horse, turn around, and look towards him. He smiles and we both crane our heads upward toward the sky. As the drops keep on falling, we grab the empty canteens and we both laugh together, freely, like two young boys without a care in the world.

The Cowboy Convinces Us of God

by John McCaine

First, my neighbor became a cowboy. Then, when his wife divorced him, he became a bandit in a mask. Overnight, he lost access to his house and became something like a raccoon.

He dug through our trash. I caught him. He denied everything in the beam of my flashlight.

A neighbor we shared, remembers once finding him dozing in her kitchen. She'd arrived late after a surprise late-shift. He was there at her kitchen table, eating cereal from a bowl. He was reading through letters she'd never read for herself. He confronted her about them, but could barely keep his eyes open. She was a widower with a longtime lover and still very ashamed.

Another mutual neighbor found him one morning asleep in the back of our neighbor's car. Our neighbor asked him to leave, admitting that, while he was sorry for his rough life up 'til now, he did not want a vagrant taking advantage of him and that, after all, it was a backseat and not a bed. 'I know how many people have the clap because of you,' said 'the bandit,' as we now referred to him. 'Here's all the evidence I need, you plague,' he said, littering the back of the man's car with handfuls of medical slips.

The cowboy once had a beautiful yard, and once had worn handsome sweaters, he had even built a treehouse in advance for the son he'd planned to have. Now he was missing many teeth and stank.

I met him for the last time, very near the very edge of his demise. He was sitting at the edge of the pool in my backyard. I was about to dive in, as I did every morning.

'Not so fast,' he said.

But I was already on the diving board. I hadn't seen him. He shook me. He'd come into my booze by luck of my unlocked sliding glass door.

'Your wife never once felt adequately loved,' he said. He held a box of things discarded I kept downstairs. He had become so hairy and could not stand on two feet.

Two Cowboys Holding Hands
by Timothy Arliss O'Brien

Many had complained to the Sheriff
But those two were still mocking this whole rodeo.

It was a strong gesture, an impassioned move.
They were even rumored to say they loved one another.

Many in the community just said they needed wives.
But they just kept going "home" together to the same farm
every night.

once, in the middle of the hottest summer on record, a few of
the guys from the stockyards
drank heavily at the tavern and tried to burn down their barn.

But this was the day the town chose hope, kindness, and love.

For you see, the community remembered all the things those
two cowboys had done for them.
Once they herded up a whole head of dairy cows, that had
escaped the double O ranch. Another time they had fixed a two
mile fence that had been damaged during a late spring tornado
right in the middle of town.

These were good cowboys, and this town knew the difference
between a hero, and a villain.

They spent all winter fixing their barn together.
And marrying in it in front of the whole town that spring.

The arsonists were charged and spent life behind bars.

Because no one harasses a good cowboy, or a couple of them.

A Spaghetti Western
This town ain't big enough for the two of us.
Yeah it is.
The End
HC

The Cowboy Thinks He's Better Than God

by John McCaine

The mayor saw how infertile we were. He organized a chain of wagons. We were to kidnap many, many children.

The rival town was known for smithing, so everywhere it smelled like metal. Our spurs sounded like rain in their concrete streets.

He built the wagons by hand. He slammed them together and ordered many cowboys inside them. He laid their insides with lambs wool closed the wheels smooth with sap. We moved in silence. If anyone talked, the mayor took his thick fingers and shushed them.

We took the children while they were sleeping, and slid them out like dolls. How did we keep them sleepy? With peaches the mayor had grown himself.

The mayor was famous for his sleeping peaches.

His hands were legendarily big. He built the buildings by lifting up their walls and holding them there while we nailed them. He dragged the tallest tree we'd ever heard of across the desert and tipped it up to be our flag pole. He killed people, if he hit them. He carried new-married men on his shoulders and pulled a baby from the burning barn. There was nothing our mayor hadn't held up.

When the children woke up, we gave them new mommies and daddies. This was a great effect to the peaches: parents had to keep feeding their children peaches to keep them always forgetting. Children grew fatter and over the years they forgot their other families completely.

Our mayor cultivated the orchard by night. He watered the trees (even in the middle of the desert, he was capable of this) and trimmed the trees. He tasted the peaches, in case of their sweetness. Nothing put him to sleep.

We told the mayor we were worried that our girls and boys would one day, no matter what, come to finally remember their parents. The peaches ensured these children would dream of their parents every night. These dreams ended in their parents devouring them.

If the parents finally found our town and made claim to their children, we'd hide their children under our houses. (The mayor had already dug the holes.)

But what if they heard their parents' voices? Then we'd stuff their ears with cotton.

One night in summer, the mayor chopped down all the peach trees. He'd seen the end of childhood coming.

He planed the tallest trees and made a prison. He put a boy who hated to sleep and was notoriously sleep-deprived in prison. He made the prison special just for the boy and opened the only window for him facing what used to be the peach grove.

The mayor took another boy from his family, who was notoriously good, and made him be guard and stand outside the prisoner's door.

The mayor taught the guard to chop wood and the two of them chopped the rest of the peach grove into firewood. He showed the guard how to tend to the furnace and keep the prisoner warm.

They seldom talked. The prisoner kept his mind on the mayor while the guard idly watched the town grow.

The mayor carved out highways and fountains. He dragged in granite from the mountains in the north and timber from the mountains in the west. There was no stopping the mayor.

On his sixteenth birthday, the boy was released from prison.

The boy got drunk and tried to light the casino on fire. They threw the boy into the street. He returned to the guard. The guard lit the furnace. They sat in the front where the guard always sat and watched an enormous statue of a god come up from the ground.

'Don't need the door anymore, do we,' joked the guard.

'I guess not,' joked the boy.

'So, what's life like on the other side?'

'No different.'

'OK,' said the guard.

The guard sat outside of the prison. He was relaxed where he sat.

'Say, what do I call you?'

The prisoner frowned at a bird.

'You don't wanna name?'

'No I do not.'

'I can give you one.'

'No, I do not want one.'

'OK,' said the guard. The guard had baked the boy a cobbler, but didn't see it fit now to give it to him.

A horse appeared in the morning. This was the last horse alive of the horses who had stolen the children. The last of the thieving horses.

The mayor was there. He was there to give a warning to the boy. His hands were worn and heavy. His hands had strangled a bear. The boy had never seen them in person before. He had seen them close when he was another person. He had seen them before he'd had any memory.

'I have broken this desert. I have broken these sands. I have constructed the impossible. And you will ruin everything.'

The boy climbed onto the horse, which the mare had reared. The mayor touched the horse and the horse seemed to tremble. He smoothed its mane.

'They will welcome you like no one ever before. You are the only son who ever returned.'

The mayor whispered something to the horse.

'You were our only criminal. The only criminal we ever had.'

The boy whipped the reins gently. The horse began their way toward the town.

BIOS

AJD
AJD has lived all over, with a few decades in the western U.S., and recommends the book *American Holocaust* by Stannard.

Michael Calkins
Michael Calkins has worked at Powell's City of Books for nearly three decades. His stories in this and previous issues of Deep Overstock are his only published work so far.

Hannah Collins
Bookseller by moonlight, photographer and comic book reader by daylight. You can find her photos on Instagram @hellokittenface.

Mickey Collins
~~Mickey rights wrongs. Mickey wrongs rites.~~ Mickey writes words, sometimes wrong words but he tries to get it write.

Ben Crowley
Ben Crowley is from Pittsburgh, Pennsylvania. He is happy to get back to writing and owes a kidney to Deep Overstock (by DHL right now, friends ;)) for getting his butt back in gear. Ben used to sort books for the Amazon warehouse, in our beautiful backcountry of western Pittsburgh. Now he drives a truck, but he's still selling books at whatever diner, truckstop or seedy hotel he finds himself in.

Robert Eversmann
Robert's website is roberteversmann.com.

Carson Everson
Carson Everson is thrilled to be a part of Deep Overstock's Westerns Journal. He likes to consider himself the last great DIY bookseller in the last frontier of the west. He runs a small honor-system bookstore on the edge of his property. The bookstore resembles a birdhouse on a pole. Take a book, leave a quarter. That's all I ask.

Desmond Everest Fuller
My name is Desmond Everest Fuller. My fiction has appeared in Rasasvada Creative and the Gorge Literary Review. I live and work in Portland, Oregon. I did work for years off and on in the fantastic bookstore, Artifacts: Good

Books and Bad Art in Hood River, Oregon.

Joe Galvan

For a year, Joe Galván sold books at a small bookstore near the Texas Tech campus in Lubbock, Texas. Born and raised on the US-Mexico border in South Texas, his work deals with the strange, shifting landscapes of time, culture and tradition. He is the author of *In The Realm of the Desert Gods*, a novel, a book of short stories entitled *Sereno* (produced for the Independent Publishing Resource Center's Certificate Program), and numerous short stories, novelettes, and essays. He is a contributor to *Texas Monthly* and *The Believer* magazine. He is fond of three things in this sad, confusing world: saints, food, and manners. He lives in Portland, Oregon.

Dan Heise

Dan Heise is a writer and actor originally from St. Louis, now living in Portland. He occasionally works at Powell's City of Books. Dan enjoys reading plays and young adult novels, and mostly enjoys writing plays and poems. His favorite part of Western movies is the music. Unsurprisingly, his favorite western movie is The Good, the Bad, and the Ugly.

Ariel Kusby

Ariel Kusby is a writer and bookseller based in Portland, Oregon. She currently works in the Rose and Orange rooms at Powell's City of Books, where she pays special attention to children's books about witches, odd cookbooks, and gnome gardening guides. You can check out her writing at www.arielkusby.com.

John McCaine

John McCaine, no relation, knows himself. He's a man of letters from Portland, Oregon, living in the West Hills. This is his parents' home and his grandparents' home. It would be his children's home too, if what happened hadn't happened. John McCaine would like to thank Deep Overstock for considering his work. John McCaine was an early investor in Walter Powell. He was also his fierce competitor. Unfortunately, McCaine books never took off. Luckily, McCaine lives off his parents' estate, now the official location of the Portland Bocce Balls Grand Tournie. He has many fine arts coffee table books, which are for sale.

Oaktea

Oaktea has always been in love with every aspect of a book--from the design to its contents, everything contributes to the experience. She started making comics for the all-in-one art and words combination, and eventually started working in bookstores to feed her voracious habit, as well as her love and respect for the form of the book itself.

Timothy Arliss O'Brien

I am an interdisciplinary artist in music composition, writing, and visual arts. My goal is to connect people to accessible new music that showcases virtuosic abilities without losing touch of authentic emotions. I have premiered music with The Astoria Music Festival, Cascadia Composers, and Sound of Late's 48 hour Composition Competition. I also want to produce writing that connects the reader to themselves in a way that promotes wonder and self realization. I have self published several novels, and have written for Look Up Records (Seattle), Our Bible App, and Deep Overstock: The Bookseller's Journal. Check out my full discography, Where Are WE?, Piano Memories, Fear Sides and Soundbath, and my newest novel, *Dear God I'm a Faggot* at my website: www.timothyarlissobrien.com

Michael Santiago

Michael Santiago is an aspiring author and current English teacher in Nanjing, China. He decided to get into education so that he could not only travel the world doing what he loves, but to ignite that creative spark by putting the power of storytelling into the hands of his students. His creative drive and passion for literature has helped him translate the power of books and their capacity to bestow knowledge onto his children.

Ben Talley

Ben Talley was raised in the humid stew of Alabama and is a pretty okay guy, despite what the cat thinks. If you speak to his grandmother, let her know that he eats regularly.

Geoff Wallin

Geoff Wallin works at Powell's City of Books doing building maintenance. He has worked as a reporter and now writes fiction for enjoyment.

Fred White

Fred D.White is a professor of English, emeritus, at Santa Clara University in northern California. His fiction, humor, and essays have appeared most recently in *Praxis*, *Wilderness House Literary Review*, *Southwest Review*, *Clockwise Cat*, *Brilliant Flash Fiction*, and *Fiction Southeast*. His books include *The Writer's Idea Thesaurus*, *Where Do You Get Your Ideas?*, *Writing Flash*, and *Approaching Emily Dickinson*. One of Fred's jobs as an undergraduate at the University of Minnesota in the '60s was working in the book department at Donaldson's Department Store (now defunct) in Minneapolis. His duties included familiarizing himself with the premises of newly released titles and working them into sales pitches. Although he quickly discovered that he was not cut out to be a salesman, being so immersed in books brought out the writer in him and turned him into a bibliophile. Over the years he assembled fine collections by and about favorite authors, especially Emily Dickinson—the latter collection proving to be immensely useful when he wrote his bibliographic study of Dickinson scholarship, *Approaching Emily Dickinson: Currents and Crosscurrents since 1960.*

Nicholas Yandell
Nicholas Yandell is a composer, who sometimes creates with words instead of sound. In those cases, he usually ends up with fiction and occasionally poetry. He also paints and draws, and often all these activities become combined, because they're really not all that different from each other, and it's all just art right?
When not working on creative projects, Nick works as a bookseller at Powell's Books in Portland, Oregon, where he enjoys being surrounded by a wealth of knowledge, as well as working and interacting with creatively stimulating people. He has a website where he displays his creations; it's nicholasyandell.com. Check it out!